The Accidental Gangster

David J. Keogh

The Accidental Gangster

David J. Keogh

Paperback Edition First Published in the United Kingdon
in 2015 aSys Publishing

eBook Edition First Published in the United Kingdon
in 2015 aSys Publishing

Disclaimer

This is a work of fiction. All characters and incidents are
products of the author's imagination and any resemblance to
actual people or events is coincidental or fictionalised.

ISBN: 978-1-910757-37-6

aSys Publishing
http://www.asys-publishing.co.uk

In the early 1960s Ronnie and Reggie Kray are the new princes of the London underworld and things are going well. Their clubs and protection rackets stretch from the East to the West end of the metropolis, but they need to expand. Hemmed in on all sides by the other ever encroaching London gangs, they need to break new ground and search further afield. They set their sights on Birmingham, Great Britain's second city. Easy pickings, or so they think.

The Fewtrells. Eight brothers who have already marked their territory and now stand alone against the vicious onslaught about to be brought down upon their heads from two of the most feared names in criminal history.

The Krays.

Based on actual events and hidden for decades. This is the story of the bloody battle for Birmingham, and perhaps the beginning of the fall of the house of Kray.

www.accidentalgangster.co.uk

Foreword

As a child growing up in Birmingham during the 1970s, I knew very little of my mother and father's involvement in the underworld. They were just Mum and Dad. Sometimes loving, sometime crazy, but always on the go. There was always someone around our house, a character from one of the clubs, or famous celebrities like Tom Jones, Lulu or Tina Turner. Dad was always on the phone with a deal going down about something or other. To me and my brother Daniel and sister Rebecca, it was just childhood, everything was hidden from us. I was eighteen before I found out who my father was, or should I say *what* my father was; whilst at University I began researching a drama project by reading about the London gang scene. My eye was drawn to a book written about the Lambrianou brothers. Purely by coincidence I opened the book at the very page that mentioned my father's name, Eddie Fewtrell, and how he had led a particularly vicious family gang from Birmingham, and how, in the early nineteen sixties the Fewtrells had put a stop to the Krays' plans to take over the city. I was shocked, but things suddenly made sense to me. My husband, the author of this book, was passed on privileged information through many in depth conversations with my father, mother and my uncles, although he has filled the blank gaps with his brilliant fiction, he probably knows more about what really happened than I do, as I say, my parents went to great lengths to protect us from their world, and it was only after I pushed my mother and father for an explanation to the writing in the Lambrianou book, that they told me the truth. So, to read this story in all it's colour and vibrance, and to feel the sixties come alive as they do on the pages of this book, I have the chance, at last, to see the world and life through the eyes of my mother and father when they were young and in their prime.

Abi Fewtrell

This book was written after many conversations with Eddie, Don, Roger, Hazel, Abigail and Daniel Fewtrell and many of the other Birmingham characters around at the time these events.

In loving memory of Hazel Fewtrell..
for Conor & Finn Keogh

Note from the Author

I believe that no one sets out to be a gangster. 99% of the people I talked to when researching this book set out to be legitimate businessmen. But life and times force situations and choices upon us that are beyond our control and in order to survive, or for the safety of family and business, sometimes, blood must be spilled. Fifty years ago life was very different, World War Two and the worst devastation the world had ever seen was still very much in the minds of the characters who play their parts in this book. Life was cheap and everyone knew it. The Sixties brought in a glimmer of light showing a life beyond the ration books and grey surroundings of a world with one foot still firmly stuck in the last days of the war. In that tiny crack of light was a vision of the future, where even a poor, working class family could become something more than they were born. Everyone could see the light and everyone wanted a slice of what it represented. Some wanted it so badly, they were prepared to kill for it.

This is a fictional story, based around real events and purely for entertainment. The actions and personalities of the characters featured in this work in no way reflect the real life characters of the same name.

Blood in the Snow

Chapter 1

That year the winter came on in a fury. Temperatures dropped so fast that anyone caught outside, like the tramps and journey men, simply froze to death where they slept off their paraffin and hair lacquer hangovers in the doorways and old bomb sites where they lay.

Even the birds which hadn't already migrated that winter were found frozen on their perches as Birmingham City Centre was transformed from its post-war Victorian decay into a landscape right from The Chronicles of Narnia.

Eddie Fewtrell rubbed his hands together gleefully. He peeked through the tiny caged lookout hatch in the thick oak studded door leading onto the snowy street outside his night club, and couldn't believe his luck. He was probably the only person in Birmingham not rubbing his hands together to get warm. The Bermuda club was packed with punters, drinking, dancing and gambling away on the makeshift poker tables. Plus it was Friday and for almost everyone in the club that meant it was payday. Meaning, they had a week's wages in their pockets and by hook or by crook Eddie was going to get every last penny out of them before the sun came up.

"We're gonna need some bacon, eggs, sausages and black pudding for the morning, 'cos these lot ain't going anywhere in this weather." He turned to the girl in the cloakroom.

"Tell Chrissy he's gonna have to go down the meat market and grab some food. Oh, and he'd better get some Irish white pudding for the Paddies too—they love that shit." The young girl scampered away into the club looking for Eddie's brother.

Eddie Fewtrell was tough, tall, blonde and handsome. In many ways he was a perfect reflection of the 1960s 'get up and go' culture. Always immaculately dressed and presented, as if to throw up a smokescreen to hide the desperate living conditions he suffered at home. The very fact he had made it this far in life was a testament to his hard roots. Eddie's mother had passed away in the last days of the 1950s leaving eleven children to fend for themselves. They lived in a terraced house in an area of Birmingham called Aston that was well below what we now call working class standards of living. His father George Fewtrell was a well-known and well-liked character. A petty criminal, infamous around Aston for his drinking and gambling, and who had lately taken to riding a horse to the pub John Wayne style. But he showed very little interest in his children.

Eddie, being one of eight brothers and two sisters, took the weight of the family on his shoulders. Like many a young man from that era, he got out in the world to make money the only way he could, selling black market goods at the Birmingham rag market. Stockings, knickers, tights, anything that couldn't be found in the shops in post war Britain. Huge crowds would assemble around him as he faked heart attacks and fits just to draw in the crowds of housewives to his stall. Screaming and shouting as if on his last breath, the women would rush over to offer help only for Eddie to leap onto his feet and burst into his hilarious flirty sales patter.

Eddie had a perfect mix of humour and ruthlessness; the ability to make people crack up laughing at his razor sharp wit, entwined with his ability to crush anyone that stood in his way without any real moral compassion. This made for a hugely charismatic young man and anyone that was in his presence knew that he was on his way to the top and nothing and no-one was going to be allowed to get in his way. "I'm not going out there, I'll fucking freeze to death!" Chrissy peeked through the hatch in the door taking in the still heavily falling snow.

"Don't be soft Chrissy. It's only down the fucking road. You can wear Don's Crombie," Eddie countered, gesturing at the cloakroom girl to pass him the coat. Chrissy reluctantly pulled the heavy camel coat on, a peeved look on his face.

Eddie pushed the club's thick oak door against the snow, half pushing, half coercing Chrissy out into the already knee-deep snow on Navigation Hill. Chrissy pulled on the overcoat that Eddie had thrown at him and began muttering complaints under his breath.

"E-ar there's a tenner. Make sure you get the white pudding for the duck eggs or they'll kick off, and another thing, don't go near that wanker Toddy Burns: he'll rip you off. He's one of the Meat Market Mob and he *fucking* hates us lot. Last thing we need is hassle from them bastards" Chrissy replied sarcastically,

"Oh fucking great. Now I'm off to enemy territory on me fucking own in a coat that's too fucking big for me in the fucking snow. I'll look a right fucking Twat."

"You don't need a coat to look like a twat our kid," Eddie replied with a snigger. With that, the door slammed and Chrissy was on his own halfway down Navigation Hill with a mile long walk ahead of him. The snow had put a stop to any taxis or cars, and even though it was 3am, for the first time since Chrissy could remember Birmingham city centre was silent and beautiful. He would have enjoyed the experience if it hadn't been for the biting wind that whipped around his ears as it blew the snowflakes into small drifts filling the door ways and gutters of the deserted streets.

Chrissy was the seventh of the eight Fewtrell boys and whatever he lacked in Eddie's confidence and business skills, he more than made up for with his fists and granite jaw. Slim and dark, he nevertheless had a right hook that could, and did, floor many a man twice his size. In another place and time he could have been a professional boxer but openings and opportunities like that were slim on the ground so he stuck with his family, his loyalty and his fists.

Birmingham Meat Market was situated just outside the City centre behind the rag market, only a stone's throw from St Martin's Cathedral. It was one of the largest and busiest wholesale markets in the country. The place would come alive around 3am as the meat and fish arrived from all over Britain to be selected and bought by the butchers and fishmongers throughout the City. Open to all the elements, and with long hours and heavy work you had to be a hard man to want to work there. But the wages were comparatively good and the social side of the job was a big reason why the barrow boys put up with such harsh conditions. With a lack of any trade unions within the market, the hardest of the men that worked there had formed a loose gang around a ring leader called Toddy Burns. This gave them a small amount of leverage against anyone that tried to move in on their patch or tried to undercut them on price. The Meat Market Mob was about 40 strong. Years of working in such conditions had made for some of the hardest men in town, Toddy Burns being the hardest of them: a six foot four bully, who was either hero-worshipped or sucked up to by everyone down the market. Toddy had a big reputation which was helped along by the rumour that he had beheaded his predecessor, in order to take over the gang. Allegedly, he had kept the head in his fridge for a month before throwing it into the victim's front garden as a halloween surprise for the poor man's widow. Anything that came through the Market had to go through the gang and they put their commission on everything even if the customers or suppliers didn't know about it. Their working day started at 2am and finished at 9am, after which most of them could be found in the Market Tavern a rough, hole in the wall pub next to the bus station and across the road from the rag market. The Market Tavern had been given a special licence by the council to serve alcohol outside of normal pub hours specifically for the meat market workers. Toddy Burns held his council there most days and whilst most folk were on their way to work in the Birmingham rush hour, it wasn't unusual to see a live band playing rock & roll at 9am to a packed house of men and women jiving and drinking to their hearts content after a hard day loading and butchering pigs, cows and sheep.

Meanwhile back at the Bermuda Club Don Fewtrell was kicking off.

"Why the fuck did you give Chrissy my coat? It's got my fucking . . . wallet in it!"

"Calm down for fuck's sake," Eddie replied dismissively, "it's not like he's gonna rob you is it?"

Eddie knew Don's temper was going to get the better of him, so he thought up a job for him to do, and sent him to tell the band to start their next set. Don gave Eddie a dark stare.

"Well you should've asked me first. It's a fucking liberty."

With that, Don stormed off through the office door and into the bar area disappearing into the smoky haze and throngs of customers. Eddie turned to Frankie shrugging. "What the fuck's got into him?"

Frankie just smiled as he always did. Frankie Fewtrell was the third brother and a real hard man with a big heart, as tough as they came but always willing to listen to the other side of the story. Unlike Don, who had a mean streak and a flair for the dramatic as far as fashion was concerned. If he liked you he could be very charming but he didn't like too many people, didn't suffer small talk, and never gave anyone second chances.

Chrissy, half-walking, half-stumbling through the deep snow reached the entrance to the Meat Market shivering in Don's oversized camel Crombie. Chrissy pulled the coat around him, pushing his hands deeper in to the pockets. But for some reason the coat seemed heavier on one side, dragging the coat out of shape. At first Chrissy couldn't find anything in the pockets that would weigh it down so much. But after a particularly dramatic icy stumble, Chrissy found a hidden pocket in the rear of the coat. In the pocket was a German Lugar pistol. Surprised by his find, Chrissy stopped and held it in his hands as if it were a thing of wonder. The pistol was old but had been well looked after and, more crucially, the magazine was full of gleaming brass cartridges. Chrissy seemed to grow another six inches, his confidence inflating as he stared at the World War two relic. He was chuffed with his find.

"The crafty bastard," he thought to himself about Don. "He's kept this quiet." If Eddie or Frankie found out he had this they'd have his guts for garters.

Eddie especially hated guns. In truth, there were plenty of World War two guns knocking around Birmingham in the early 1960s. Chrissy had seen and fired plenty of them on the old bomb sites around the city. Old Berettas and Brownings were quite common but he had never come across a German Luger before.

"It really is a thing of beauty," he thought, "like something out of a Bond film."

"OI you! What's your game? This is private property." A voice came from a small shed at the entrance to the Meat Market, as a security guard in an old tatty uniform stepped into the snow.

"Alright mate, I'm after some bacon and stuff for the Bermuda club up the road."

The Guard looked at him as if he were insane. Sarcastically, he turned to the empty Market with his arms outstretched, emphasising that the place was shut due to the snow.

"Are you fucking blind? There ain't no bacon here today," he said laughing, "they're all down the Tavern getting pissed mate. You might find someone down there that's got a van with something to sell but it's all shut here as you can see." With that the guard stepped back inside his little shed, slamming the door. Chrissy stood there feeling stupid. The snow was falling heavier now and the wind had a chill in it that cut through the thick material of the coat. Cursing his Italian Loafers which seemed to soak up the snow with every step and freezing his toes, he smiled to himself.

"The Market Tavern, well at least I can have a whisky and warm myself up."

The thought of a hot Toddy whisky warming his cockles spurred him on and he began the trudge through the white silent streets towards the Market Tavern.

Things were in full swing at the Tavern. The bands usually didn't show up until 8am, so in lieu of a live band one of the barmaids was playing whatever records she could find in the landlord's collection on a portable Dansett record player. With its volume turned up as far as it could go, it distorted the Rock & Roll and Beat music making most of the songs unrecognisable, but that didn't stop people twisting on the tiny dance floor. As a matter of fact the atmosphere was buzzing. The snow had brought an unexpected holiday and the partygoers were going to make the best of it. The air sat thick with cigarette smoke creating a white haze that hid the darker corners of the pub and in one of those dark corners sat Toddy and his right hand man Duncan Jarvis. Jarvis was lean, wiry, with not an ounce of fat on him. He had a spiteful, sharp cruel face, a shock of red hair in a greasy quiff and a thick drawn out Liverpool accent. Jarvis was well known around the market as a man not to cross. Most of the workers turned a blind eye to his taste for young lads. Love and Nancy-boy cuddles weren't for him. He enjoyed the struggle and the look of shock on the face of his young rape victims. He had thrown away any idea of discretion years ago when he served in the merchant navy and had given himself over to hedonistic violent, and in a couple of cases deadly, sex whenever the opportunity presented itself. Unlike the majority of homosexuals in Birmingham at the time, he avoided the gay bars and clubs unless it was to see his dealer for some French blues or Dexies. The amphetamines were popular around the clubs and he used them to lure the unsuspecting young Mods boys back to his digs in Moseley, one of the more avant-garde areas of the city. But the most important thing as far as Toddy was concerned was that Duncan Jarvis gave his unconditional loyalty to Toddy and in return it was said, Toddy repaid that loyalty with first pick of the foster kids his wife took in from Birmingham City Council.

The second Chrissy Fewtrell swung the glass doors of the tavern open and stepped in to the noisy bar, Jarvis's gaze was drawn to him. Chrissy stood just inside the door giving himself a second or two for his vision to adjust to the thick eye watering cigarette smoke.

"Hey big boy, look what the cat's dragged in." Jarvis said, tugging Toddy's elbow. They watched as the young man walked across the bar dodging the dancers and began a conversation with the Landlord.

"Alright mate, I'm after some bacon and stuff for the Bermuda club up the road. Anyone selling?" asked Chrissy, half-shouting in the landlord's face over the music. The landlord just pointed in the general direction of Toddy Burns.

"Ask him, the big bloke. He's the boss of 'em. Anything else I can get ya?"

"Yea I'll have a hot Toddy, it's fucking freezing out there," Chrissy said putting on a false shiver to emphasise the weather he'd walked through.

"Right up son, but mind your language," said the landlord, pointing at an old yellowing smoked stained bakelite sign behind the bar with the words, *No Blacks, No Irish, No Dogs, No Gypsies, No Foul Language.* written on it. Chrissy gave a shrug and the landlord turned and began preparing the drink. Chrissy slapped a pound note down on the bar.

"Don't worry handsome. I'll get that." Jarvis put his hand on Chrissie's and closed his fist around the money.

"Cheers," Chrissy replied, pulling the drink towards him.

"So what brings you in here then luv, lost in the snow?"

Chrissy had trouble understanding the Scouse accent but eventually replied,

"Nah I'm after some bacon and breakfast stuff for our lot up at the Bermuda club on Navigation Street. Do you know if anyone's got anything to sell in one of the vans?"

Jarvis stepped back, his smile dropping. He looked over at the girl by the record player and gave her a shake of his head. With that, the music stopped and the dancers were left throwing strange shapes on the dance floor in silence for a few seconds. Slowly almost everyone in the pub turned to see what the reason for the silence was. Chrissy looked around the pub; an uneasy feeling beginning to grow in his stomach, his smile hanging uselessly.

"He's from the Bermuda club. After some bacon and stuff." There was a shuffling of tables and stools being pushed back.

"The fucking Bermuda club!" came a huge voice out of the smoky darkness. "Is he a fucking Fewtrell?"

Jarvis turned to Chrissy. "Are you a fucking Fewtrell?" he asked softly. Chrissy peered through the darkness trying to make out the owner of the deep voice a feeling of dread washing over him.

"Yea I'm a fucking Fewtrell. What of it?"

The deep voice stepped out of the shadows onto the dance floor.

"I'll tell you what of it. Your fucking brother shagged my sister then sacked her from his club!"

Toddy Burns stood full height pointing at Chrissy, his finger only inches away from his face.

"You tell that cunt when I see him I'll fucking tear him a new arsehole."

Chrissy was taken aback by the instant aggression.

"Which brother? I've got seven of 'em." he said, pulling himself together. In truth Chrissy wasn't fazed by Toddy Burns. He had knocked out bigger men than him. His main concern was the amount of men he'd have to fight if it kicked off. But he'd had a few good hidings in his time, and it looked like he was about to get another one tonight. He took a step straight into Toddy's face.

"You don't need excuses with me mate. I'm not interested in your slag of a sister. By the look of you, you've probably shagged her yourself. If you want a pop at me just do it and see what fucking happens."

Toddy was shocked. People didn't stand up to him very often and if they did they soon backed down when some of his Meat Market boys backed him up. But this lad wasn't backing down to anyone. Toddy found himself in a position he didn't relish. If he didn't do something he would lose the respect that kept his gang under control. If he did make a move on this lad he might get more than he bargained for. But like all bullies and cowards, what he lacked in courage he more than made up for in volume.

"You're a fucking dead man standing and you don't even know it. You think you can come in here and threaten *ME!* When I'm finished beating you I'm gonna give you to Jarvis and he's gonna shag your arse. Then you'll understand how my sister feels you fucking toe rag." Toddy grabbed Chrissy around the neck and pulled him in close. He was expecting to see fear in Chrissy's eyes, but instead he saw defiance. He increased his grip, trying to strangle the look out of the young man's eyes. He snarled into Chrissy's face baring his teeth. Chrissy could smell the nicotine and alcohol mixing with the smell of halitosis on Toddy's breath as the men stood toe to toe. But the look on Toddy's face slowly began to change from anger to shock as the barrel of the Lugar pistol jabbed into his ribs.

"Come on Toddy fucking have him. I want my turn!" Jarvis's slimy voice rang out across the pub. Chrissy slid the gun up to Toddy's neck, pointing the gun vertically under his chin.

"You die first. Get it. The rest might get me in a rush but not before your brains are a stain all over the fucking ceiling. Understand?" A silence came over the group of men who had gathered around the dance floor to watch the action as they caught a first glimpse of the gun.

"He's bluffing. Fucking have him!" came a voice from the crowd. Chrissy pulled back the hammer on the pistol.

"No, back off, he ain't bluffing," Toddy shouted, fear now growing in his eyes.

"He thinks he's the only one with a gun!" someone shouted.

"Back off!" Toddy screamed, "he'll fucking do it!"

Chrissy smiled. "Now you and me are gonna take a stroll over to the door and I'll say goodnight."

He raised his voice so everyone in the pub could hear.

"Anyone that steps outside that door or tries to follow me, I'll shoot you in the street like a fucking dog. Don't think I won't do it either." With that, Chrissy, without taking his eyes off of Toddy's face, reached across the bar, grabbed the whisky Jarvis had bought him and downed it. Nodding his head towards the glass doors, he motioned Toddy to start moving out of the bar.

"Goodnight ladies, cheers for the drink."

Chrissy pushed the glass door open. As the two men stepped into the street Toddy made his move. Grabbing Chrissy's arm and pushing the gun away from his face, he locked his other hand around Chrissy's throat and tried to twist him against the wall of the pub. But the snow gave no traction beneath their feet and the two of them crashed to the ground. Toddy lost his grip as he fell and smashed his mouth on the cold concrete step on the entrance to the bar. The men inside the pub began to slowly, cowardly peek through the steamy glass doors and Chrissy, realising he didn't have much time before they plucked up enough guts to rush him, was the first to lift himself off the pavement still holding the gun in his right hand. Toddy looked up and snarled, his teeth covered in blood.

"You fucking basta! . . ." he began to say, when Chrissy brought the butt of the Lugar down hard across Toddy's nose, breaking it and sending his head back into the concrete, knocking him out cold. The men inside finally found their courage and began to push the glass doors onto the street. Thankfully for Chrissy, the doors opened outwards and Toddy's head was in the way. Toddy began to stir. Chrissy took one look at the angry men, now screaming for blood, and legged it down the street as best he could in the snow.

Inside the bar, the room was in chaos as the group tried to force the doors open, shouting abuse through the pane glass windows as the young man in the oversized Crombie made his escape. Toddy's head spun. Punch drunk, he could hear the swirling screaming of his friends through the doors and little by little he regained his awareness. Lifting himself from the snow he looked down at what seemed like cupfuls of thick gleaming crimson blood pouring out of his nose onto the pure white snow, forming a small steaming puddle of crystal red before spreading into the frozen whiteness. He stared at the stain for a few seconds, captivated by its gory beauty. As Toddy stood up swaying, they helped him back inside the pub, sitting him at a table. The room fell silent and a large glass of whisky was slammed down in front of him. Toddy raised the glass to his lips, his hands shaking with adrenalin and rage. The men waited to see what Toddy would say.

"What you lot fucking looking at? What was I meant to do? He had a fucking gun! Put the fucking music back on, there's been enough drama tonight," he shouted at the barmaid. A small murmur arose around the bar as the men began to talk of revenge. The barmaid hesitantly turned on the Dansette, looking for reassurance from the landlord.

"Don't worry about that bastard," Toddy shouted. "We'll settle this properly by taking the whole lot of them Aston sewer rats down." He looked around the smoky bar at the men's faces. Toddy knew that if he didn't show strength now he would lose control. He searched the faces of the men looking for some back up, but the face he was searching for was missing. Jarvis had taken advantage of the drama and disappeared behind the bar and out through the pub's cellar door which opened up on the street fifty yards further up from where Chrissy had made his escape. He reached the doors just as Chrissy was passing.

"Night night dear," he half-whispered. "I'll be seeing you real soon." The voice made Chrissy jump. He still had the gun in his hand and he pointed it at the shadow. He couldn't make out who was there and he wasn't going to hang around to find out either. Suddenly the shadow was illuminated as the headlamps of a small red and white Comor van pulled up on the snowy street. The shadow raised his hands and waved effeminately at Chrissy.

Chrissy could see the greasy red quiff and sharp jaw line of Duncan Jarvis bathed in the van's lights. The passenger door of the van slid back and a young lad gestured to Chrissy, shouting in a thick Irish accent.

"Come on for feck sake get in. If them lot come out and catch ye they'll fecking skin ye alive."

Chrissy didn't hesitate. Leaping across the snow pile in the gutter he threw himself onto leather bench seat in the van's cab. The little van's engine roared as best it could and its wheels dug into the fresh snow, finally finding some traction and pushing the van across the white road. Chrissy grabbed the sliding door and slammed it shut. The van was careering sideways up the street but gradually the driver brought the van under control, and as Jarvis watched the little van disappearing into the snow storm, he thought to himself that a red and white Comer butcher's van wouldn't be too hard to track down. If he couldn't get to Chrissy, then he would track down this little Irish hero and make him pay for his loyalty to the Fewtrells.

"Fucking hell Higgins, perfect timing our kid!"

Relief washed over Chrissy as the two men broke out into uncontrollable laughter. Higgins had been watching the proceedings from the end of the bar and slunk out when things had started to get heated. His father owned two butcher's shops along the old Coventry road either end of Small Heath, supplying the huge Irish community that lived there. Higgins had protested about driving in the snow but his father had forced him out into the cold to buy whatever meat was available. "Are ye still after some bacon and stuff?" Chrissy nodded laughing at the ridiculousness of the question.

"Yea. I need some white pudding too. You Paddys love it apparently." Both men were laughing hysterically by now. As the Comer van crossed the city centre, Higgins reflected on the night's events,

"Tonight was just a case of being in the right place at the right time and doing the right thing by a mate," he thought proudly to himself. But his actions would have consequences that would catch up with him in ways he couldn't imagine, even in his worst nightmares.

The new lords of London

Chapter 2

The house was a huge Georgian affair, sitting mid-terrace on Wycombe Square, Chelsea. The rooms were full of exotic antiquities, gilt French furniture and portraits of long dead ancestors alongside framed photographs showing politicians and film stars. The place just oozed old money. A soft yellow glow of candles illuminated the writhing semi-naked bodies sprawled around the richly decorated ground floor. The groans of men pierced the elegant classical music being performed by a string quartet playing to themselves at the foot of the sweeping stair case in the huge entrance hall.

The men came from all walks of life. Judges, politicians, city speculators, soldiers, heroes, villains, even pop stars; all had a role to play. The one thing they all had in common was their *illegal* sexual attraction to people of the same sex. The host of the party and owner of the house was a man in his late fifties called Lord Boothby. Well known as one of Britain's most passionate politicians he also had an insatiable appetite for homosexual adventure and his parties were already infamous in London's high society circles. Anyone with a taste for his type of sexual hedonism was searched out and invited to participate in his very own personal Roman orgies. Boys recruited and groomed from borstal homes all over the country were barely in their teens, and were plied with drinks and made to perform sex acts on men who referred to the children as *Boothby's puppies.*

Ronnie Kray watched bored as one of the party goers had difficulty trying to train a particularly pretty blond puppy. Ronnie wasn't really into this type of thing. Make no mistake, he liked boys, but he just liked them a little bit older. Sixteen to twenty, that was the age when a lad knew what he wanted and knew how to give it and take it. Ronnie was one of two twins. He had a flair for the dramatic, a taste for the exotic, and a touch some would say of the psychotic. He was unlike his brother Reggie, who was a bit (shall we say) less passionate about violence than he was. Ronnie got his kicks from starting the fight but it was Reggie who would usually finish it. Ronnie didn't rub his homosexual life in Reggie's face. Reggie didn't ask and Ronnie didn't tell. The twins' beloved mother always knew Ronnie was a bit different. Chastising him to date girls like his brother, Ronnie protested and her laughing reply would always be "Two Ron's don't make a Reg," But he knew she was proud of the business they had fought for and won. He knew that she took pride in the fact that it was her little princes that had driven out the Italian, Irish and Greek mobs that ran the snooker and gambling clubs around the east end of London. She never asked how they had done it though, and any rumours of the sick violence that her boys laid out were quickly silenced. The people there now showed her respect and that was good enough reward for him. Anyway here he was, an East End boy mixing with the cream of society. They had come a long way and this was just the beginning.

He sat in the huge green leather arm chair in the study of the mansion drinking a particularly smooth whisky that he couldn't pronounce the name of. His mind was floating in and out of the proceedings taking place in front of him. The man he was watching was trying to coerce the lad to perform oral sex on him but the blonde wasn't having any of it and putting up a fight that the man in his late fifties wasn't prepared for. In truth Ronnie could see something in the lad that reminded him of himself. The boy was telling the man to.

"Go suck your own cock!" and making fun at the size of the small penis that the man was drunkenly trying to push into his face. The boy was obviously either drunk or had been drugged but Ronnie liked the fight in the kid.

"Go on my son" he said half laughing, "you tell the old cunt where to go."

The BBC executive looked across the room to where Ronnie was sitting and was about to protest at the outburst. But when the man saw who was behind the East End accent he quickly looked back at the boy, slapping him as hard as he could around the face. "Stop fucking around and open your filthy little mouth."

The man shouted, feeling his humiliation growing. The boy reeled back at the slap. His sky blue eyes were wide open now as the reality that this was no longer a game slowly dawned on him. The other boys in the room gradually stopped what they were doing and turned to see what the commotion was all about. The man realised that he was now the centre of attention, which made him even more sexually aroused and as the men and the other boys watched he set about his puppy with a string of blows to the child's head. Ronnie sat up, the action finally getting his attention.

"Facking hell son. You're not going to let the old cant get away with that are ya?"

The boy placed his arms across his head cradling his skull from the weakening blows. He looked sideways at Ronnie, their eyes locking for a second. The blonde saw a look of sympathy in Ronnie's eyes and he answered it with one of defiance. Ronnie gestured him to fight back by holding his hands in a boxer's stance. Although the shower of blows had only lasted a few seconds the BBC executive, who had spent years sitting at his desk in Maida Vale studios, was not the fittest of men and was growing weary of his violent burst of energy. The boy waited for the blows to slow down, and as fast and as hard as he could he brought his fist up straight into the man's balls. The executive squealed, grabbing his groin and, knees buckling under him, he fell crumpled on the floor in a foetal position.

Ronnie burst into laughter, slapping the arm of the green leather chair and knocking the cut-glass onto the floor.

"Yes my san! Now facking finish him off!" The boy stood looking at Ronnie for some assurance, a smirk growing on his face. Ronnie continued,

"Go on boy, to the head," he gestured a kick with his right foot. The boy walked back about ten feet. His naked body showed signs of previous beatings he had received at other parties. He ran at the crumpled figure on the floor, his right foot striking the man's head as if he were scoring a goal on a Saturday afternoon football match. The man's head lifted from the floor with the force of the kick, a soft groan coming from him as his arms instinctively shot up to protect his head. The other boys stood in silent horror, in the realisation that a mutiny like this would mean beatings for all of them. The boy walked back across the room to retake the kick. But as he did the lights came on.

"What in god's name is going on?" Lord Boothby stood in the doorway, hands on hips, sweaty shirt sleeves rolled up to his elbows, and looking as if he had just run a mile. Ronnie rose out of his chair, the bright chandelier bringing him back in to reality. He looked sheepishly around the room as if *he* were one of the guilty schoolboys that surrounded him.

"Eh well . . . we was just having a bit of fan and it got out of hand, didn't it boys?" The youngsters nodded to each other trying to hide their smirks. Lord Boothby saw the crumpled man and let out a gasp.

"Jonty, my dear man what have they done to you?" The BBC man groaned and tried to stand, only managing to kneel with his hands still between his legs.

"That little bastard punched me in the balls!" he said gesturing with his head towards the blonde.

"Then he kicked me in the head!" The boy looked at Boothby, his blue eyes starting to fill. Boothby looked perplexed.

"Did you ask him to punch you in the balls and kick you in the head dear boy? I didn't think you were into that sort of thing?" The man's face screwed up.

"Of course I didn't you fool. It was him over there," he nodded at Ronnie. "he encouraged him to do it. We all told you not to mix with his type."

The smile dropped from Ronnie and Boothby's face in the same instant.

"Who you calling *his type?"* Ronnie crossed the room before the man could finish his sentence. He grabbed the man by the hair pulling his head sideways so that their faces were only inches away from each other.

"It's *my type* that run this facking city now *Jonty* old chum." He virtually spat the words into the man's face. "And you'd do well to remember it." He slapped the man hard with the back of his hand bringing a small trickle of blood from the man's mouth. Ronnie could feel that familiar feeling rising in his head, making the room spin. He knew the red mist was coming; it had happened hundreds of times before and he was ready to give himself over to it.

"Whatever's going to happen, then so be it and fack the consequences," he thought. "These fackers must show some respect."

The man in front of him knelt cowering in terror, flinching from Ronnie's words, too scared to even try and free himself from the grip on his hair. Then from somewhere right next to Ronnie came a soft familiar voice. Two hands softly touched his shoulders, soothing the rising menace out of him.

"Ronnie . . . Ronnie darling," hands on his face now softly caressing him. "Don't do anything silly Ronnie. Calm down dear." He could hear the voice now and it was Boothby's.

Ronnie broke his gaze with the BBC man and turned his head to Lord Boothby who took his hands and cradled Ronnie's face. The rage slowly dissipated and Ronnie turned full toward Boothby standing there for a second paralysed in the other man's arms. Then Ronnie pulled the man into him and kissed him full on his mouth. The two men stood embraced in passion for what seemed like a full minute as the room full of boys and men watched in silence. The tension in the room passed, and the others went back to what they had been doing before the drama started.

Boothby held out his hand to Jonty and the man struggled to his feet.

"Now, gentlemen, I think you two should forget this silly misunderstanding and shake hands." Ronnie and Jonty looked sheepishly at each other, fear still in the BBC man's eyes as he held out his hand.

"No hard feelings pal." Ronnie gave the man's hand a squeeze.

"There, water under the bridge all friends now, eh?" said Boothby turning and leaving the room, gesturing Ronnie to join him. The two men held hands as they reached the entrance hall of the building. "Ronnie my dear boy, we can't have any of your East End shenanigans happening here you know," Boothby looked into Ronnie's eyes. "You know I'm very fond of you but I just can't have any scandals happening to me right now." Ronnie knew that Boothby was referring to a Sunday paper article questioning wisdom of a politician of Lord Boothby's standing mixing with the likes of the Kray twins. "I understand your lordship," Ronnie said sarcastically. "I'll get my coat." Boothby put his hand on Ronnie's shoulder.

"Yes, it might be best if we don't see each other for a week or two."

Ronnie nodded and walked across the marble entrance hall to the coat stand. The band continued to play and Boothby's guest continued to cavort as Ronnie stepped out into the morning sunrise. He checked his watch and was shocked to see it was already 7.30am. Where had the night gone? He searched in his pocket for some more french blues but found none. He had been taking far too much of the speed lately anyway and was sure that was the reason he was having problems getting aroused around his boyfriends. A gun metal Jaguar pulled up at the curb, its chrome gleaming against the sunrise, and the V8 engine purring softly. A tall, heavy set man stepped out and opened the back door of the car.

"Morning Mr Kray," he said with a thick East End accent and a toothless smile.

"Morning Stan. Take me home, I need some sleep. I'm facking knackered." Ronnie collapsed onto the red leather bench seat in the rear of the car. He was meant to be in a meeting this morning with the Yanks but Reggie would have to deal with it on his own. Reggie was better at that type of thing. Ronnie would always lose his temper, flying off the handle and nothing would be achieved, and this meeting was more important than the others. The Americans were putting forward a business deal and wanted the boys to be part of it. The twins felt very proud that they were even considered to partner up with the New York mob, but he was too tired now to even consider going to the meeting.

"Eah Stan, have a look in the glove box an' see if there's any Valium?" Stan's huge hands opened the mahogany glove box door and passed a small bottle back to Ronnie. He emptied the bottle into his hand, slipped two pills into his mouth and, reaching over to the cut glass decanter that sat precariously on the drinks shelf in the middle of the car, took a deep swig of whisky, swallowing the pills along with the golden liquid. The whisky wasn't like Lord Boothby's. It stung the back of his throat, but gave him a warm feeling in his chest, relaxing him instantly. He lay across the red leather as the car travelled effortlessly across the city, watching his beloved London streets come to life in the early winter morning, his eyes and mind slowly succumbing to the Valium.

Someone on the Inside

Chapter 3

Winter's frozen grip finally released Birmingham on the third day. The cold spell was over as the thaw turned the city centre from its fairytale whiteness into a brown-grey sludge resembling the battle fields of the Somme. Huge piles of old brown snow lined the roads leading into the city, sloshing in the gutters and soaking pedestrians who were unlucky enough to be standing at the roadside as buses and cars drove through the slush, sending plumes of frozen water sloshing over the pavements.

No-one at the Bermuda club had any idea just how serious Friday night's incident was. There were two reasons for this. Firstly, Eddie and Frankie were total optimists who never took any situation too seriously. Yes, Chrissy had mentioned something about Toddy Burns but, and this brings us to our second point, Chrissy didn't want to make too much of a big deal about it, partially because with the discovery of the gun, he now had something on Don. This would be a favour he would take great delight in calling in at some point in the future. Chrissy didn't mention the secret pocket or the Lugar because if he had, Eddie would have exploded at having guns around the club. He just handed the coat back to Don with a knowing wink. Don took the coat sheepishly with the smallest of nods and disappeared into the club before anything could be said.

Eddie wasn't scared of guns, or opposed to using them when needs must. He just didn't see the point in risking being found with one in the club at the moment. He was in the middle of a battle with the town council and their henchmen, Birmingham city police, and when a raid came, as he knew it would, he didn't want another reason for them to shut him down before he'd started. Eddie had taken over the run down little pub on Navigation Hill and transformed it into a 24 hour speakeasy with dance floor, stage and gambling tables. He had never bothered applying for the proper licence for what was now the Bermuda club. If he had they would have simply turned him down.

The middle class councillors took great delight in keeping families like the Fewtrells in their place. Eddie had tried lots of entrepreneurial ideas over the past few years since being discharged from the army. But working on a market stall in the rag market selling lingerie that he had long-firmed from various legitimate suppliers just wasn't going to cut it. Up until now he had managed to keep the wolf at the door by literally barring the council from entering, hence the thick oak studded door to the club. He would peer out through the little wrought iron cage that covered the small hatch in the door and decide who was coming in and who wasn't. But he knew that it was just a matter of time before they raided the club.

On the up side, a few months previously, he had a stroke of good luck thanks to his father George. George had never had much to do with his kids before the Bermuda club. But now thanks to the free beer, he saw them nearly every night. With his horse tethered up in the side street, George could be found at one of the tables drinking and betting cash he didn't have. But like all good sons, Eddie or one of the other brothers would bail him out or every now and again explain to the other gamblers in very harsh terms that the score couldn't be settled, and they had better forget about whatever it was that George owed.

On one particularly boozy night the club was quiet, so Eddie decided to shut early around 1am. Eddie and Frankie helped the (by now legless) George outside to his awaiting mare, pushing him into the old saddle and placing his feet in the stirrups. Eddie gave the horse's arse a good slap and the old nag began its journey back to Aston.

"That horse knows Birmingham better than he does!" Frankie said, laughing as the old man clip-clopped up the street, silhouetted by the yellow street lights. The two brothers turned to re-enter the club when in the distance, to their surprise, they heard another horse's hooves coming up the hill in the other direction. Turning back, they saw a large white horse galloping up Navigation Hill with a police officer holding on for dear life. The horse was clearly out of control and the uniformed man on his back was struggling to pull the animal up.

"Ei ei here's the fucking cavalry!" Eddie said, laughing. The policeman rode past them, straining on the reins and almost lying across the horse's back trying to halt the creature. As he passed the two men, their eyes met and Eddie could see a look of total panic in the officer's eyes.

"Evening, constable!" Eddie shouted sarcastically.

"Nice evening for a ride." Frankie burst into laughter as the horse raced by them, catching up with George's little mare at the top of the hill. George didn't know what hit him. One minute he was sleeping soundly to the soft clip-clop of his ride home as he had done hundreds of times before. The next thing, he had a horse's head on his shoulder as the white steed with the policeman still on top tried to mount the mare, with George caught in-between the two. The white horse grabbed George's coat in his mouth biting into the old donkey jacket and pinning him onto the saddle. Screaming riders, snorting neighing horses and hysterical laughter from the two brothers filled the street as what seemed like a circus act performed up and down the slippery road. Every time George screamed, Eddie and Frankie burst out into uncontrollable belly laughs, gripping their sides and tears rolling down their faces.

After what seemed like an hour to the riders, but was in reality just a few minutes, the white steed did his business and began to calm down. The brothers were by now curled in balls of laughter on the floor. The policeman had dismounted and was calming his horse down and George, who was still in a state of shock and still screaming in a high pitched horror movie style, was, due to a broken girth strap, now dangling precariously beneath his nag; he was still in the saddle thanks to his feet being trapped in his stirrups. The policeman tied his horse to the iron railings and crossed the street. He looked at the other horse who was now just standing in the middle of the road knees buckled and in shock and asked, "Where's the rider gone?"

Eddie pointed beneath the mare's flank saying, "Who do you mean, *Hop-a-Long fucking Cassidy*?" The brothers burst into laughter again. The policeman smiled and walked to the side of the horse, instinctively grabbing its reins. Frankie and Eddie were waiting, breath held, to see what the officer would say. Squatting down on his haunches until his face was level with the poor inverted George he said in his best *Dixon of Dock Green* voice,

"Good evening Sir. Are you the owner of this horse?" All three men exploded into hysterical laughter once more. The policeman rolled on to in his back in the road giggling, and slapped his thigh along with the two brothers who were both collapsed against the building guffawing.

Twenty minutes later all four men were sat inside the Bermuda club drinking tea. Frankie had some sausages sizzling, and the four were about to set into some door step sandwiches. Every now and again a snigger would set them all of again, but slowly they all began to relax. Eddie liked the policeman instantly. Normally he had no time for the law but this lad was different.

He was young for a start and had only been in the job a few weeks. To Eddie this was a golden opportunity not to be missed.

"How long you been riding horses then?" he asked offering another sandwich to the officer.

"Obviously not long enough," he replied shrugging his shoulders, "I didn't even want to ride fucking horses. I wanted to be a detective but they only had spaces in the mounted police so I went for it." Frankie sat himself down at the office table tea in hand,

"Where you from? That ain't a Brummie accent is it?" The young man smiled,

"Gloucester mate. I suppose you city boys would think I'm a country bumpkin."

George sat looking dissatisfied at his dark red tea.

"Ain't you got something a bit stronger, son?" he said without breaking his gaze at the steaming cup. Eddie shook his head and raised his eyes to the ceiling.

"I'm in shock!" the old man continued.

"I think the horse had more of a shock than you did!" Frankie said, looking at Eddie. The laughter started again.

"What's your name, our kid?" Eddie interjected in to the laughter. The policeman stood up putting his sandwich down on the old china plate offering his hand to Eddie.

"God, I'm sorry I should've introduced myself. Chris Dix, my mates just call me Dixie but I ain't got too many mates here yet. They're a right bunch of stuck up bastards down at Steelhouse Lane nick. I'm thinking of knocking it on the head and going back to Gloucester." Eddie grabbed his hand and shook it firmly.

"Nah don't do that mate, stick it out. It'll all come good in the end. I'm Eddie, this is Frankie, and *John Wayne* over there is our dad." George raised his hand without looking at the policeman. Frankie just continued to eat his thick white sandwich.

"If you don't want to ride horses I might be able to help you."

The policeman sat back down a serious look removing the smile from his face.

"Oh yea, how are you gonna do that, then?" Eddie leant over the table and half whispered,

"You scratch my back I'll scratch yours. Simple."

Frankie put his food down and began to pay attention. Eddie was making a move on the copper and Frankie hadn't seen it coming. Eddie was fast to see an opportunity but even faster to take advantage of it once one arose.

"If I hear about anything going on that could help your career I'll let you know." Dixie smirked.

"Mmm . . . what type of thing? And what would you want in return?" he asked, raising his brow.

"All I'm asking you to do is return the favour. Just let me know if you hear something that involves me or the club. That's all I'm after."

The policeman shook his head.

"I don't know, I mean if they found out down the station." Eddie butted in,

"For instance, if you went back to the station tonight and told them you knew who was responsible for the recent jewellery warehouse break-ins that have been happening in Hockley, and you had names and addresses of who and where the stuff was being fenced, well I'd say you would be a bit of a hero around the police bar tomorrow night wouldn't you?"

Frankie couldn't believe his ears. Eddie was about to help the police nick one of their own. The officer's brow furrowed, confused. "I don't even know about any jewellery break-ins?"

Eddie pretended to be surprised.

"Really. Well, the rest of the nick know about it alright. They've been trying to catch whoever's responsible for months now. Imagine if *you* could solve it, our kid. They wouldn't have you riding fucking horses then would they!"

The idea was beginning to sound attractive to Dixie.

"How would I explain to them where I got the names, though?"

Eddie walked across to a set of small shelves and pulled a bottle of scotch from behind some books. Pulling the cork out with his teeth, he grabbed four glasses and sat back down handing out the glasses to all around the table.

"Just tell them you've got your sources and don't let them push you on who it is. Tell them you've got your ear to the ground and you've got plenty of other stuff too."

They sat in silence for a few seconds letting Dixie think about what was on the cards. Eddie glanced down at his stolen Rolex watch and smiled,

"Have we got a deal then?" He raised his glass to the young policeman. Dixie smiled, stood up, and raised his too, clinking it with the other men.

"I've got a feeling this is the start of a beautiful friendship," he said.

"Now, Eddie tell me about these jewellery break-ins, I'm all ears!"

Declaration

Chapter 4

Duncan Jarvis sat on the little silver GS Vespa outside The Shamrock Butcher's store on the Old Coventry Road. The little red and white Comer van had only taken him a few days to track down. The snow had slowed the search but now Jarvis was sitting watching the young Irish hero that had rescued Chrissy Fewtrell from a good beating the other night load pig carcasses onto his shoulder and carry them into the shop. Jarvis took pleasure in the fact that Higgins was living on borrowed time. He kicked the silver scooter into life, its pap-pap-pap blowing a cloud of sweet smelling purple smoke into the cold air. He turned the handlebars and headed back into the city centre. Toddy would be very happy with him, maybe even reward him with something special from the foster home. He had a tingle running around his body and a premonition of what was in store for the young butcher boy running through his head. Finding him was one thing, grabbing him off the street was another. He had organised people, and a place for the punishment. Somewhere he'd used before. Somewhere that stifled the sound of screams and a spot of bondage or torture wouldn't stand out too much. The landlord of the Trocadero pub hadn't been too happy about it but wouldn't say no to Toddy. All Jarvis had to do now was clear it with the big man and put things in motion.

The Trocadero was Birmingham's front line gay bar. The pub was a regular drop off point for the police for a bit of queer bashing. But the homosexuals that drank there were a resilient lot. The front bar was a filthy affair caught in the Victorian era and looked like that was the last time it had seen a cleaning. The tobacco-stained ceiling dripped dirty brown spots of old stinking tobacco on to the shoulders of the men underneath on any one of Birmingham's rare warm nights.

Homosexuality was still illegal so the openly flamboyant drag queens hadn't yet come onto the scene. But Shirley Bassey or Doris Day could be heard playing on a gramophone from behind the bar and someone would always be walking the room miming the words to the songs. The back bar was only for friends of the landlord, and if you went through the back bar it led to the cellar of the pub, a cavernous room that felt more like a World War Two bunker than a storage room. With a low ceiling and without windows, it just had a small steel trap door leading to the street above. From there the beer barrels were rolled down the wooden slide onto the coconut matting sacks placed there to catch their fall.

The room wasn't somewhere you would choose to spend the last twenty four hours of your life. But four days after Jarvis spotted Higgins outside the Shamrock butcher's store, that's exactly where Higgins found himself. We will never really know what happened in that cellar. But we do know that afterwards Higgins' body was found dumped in the street outside the Bermuda club. The Coroner stated at the post-mortem he had suffered several amputations. He had also been sodomised a number of times and the coroner had found a large amount of Amphetamine in what was left of his blood stream. If this was in his blood stream before he was snatched or force fed to him by his capturers we will never know. What is certain is that the speed pumping around his body kept him conscious for the whole twenty four hours of torture, buggery and amputation, before his heart finally exploded and brought what must have been the blessing of death to the innocent young man.

Eddie had heard of the body being found only an hour after it had been dumped on Navigation Hill. The Birmingham jungle drums spread the word throughout the city faster than the local paper ever could. He knew about the murder, but nobody knew who it was or why they had been killed. Eddie and Chrissy arrived at the club around seven. Dixie had tipped him off to the fact that the two detectives in charge of the murder case wanted to talk to them both. Eddie had protested that just because the body was found outside his club didn't mean he or his brothers had anything to do with it. But Dixie had told them the detectives were coming like it or not and he had better close the club for the night. Eddie reluctantly agreed.

The crowds of police and journalists had all gone by the time the black cab pulled up on Navigation Hill. The dried blood had been washed away and things looked as they should. The two brothers entered the club. Chrissy made them both some tea and they sat facing each other in the main bar area to wait for the coppers.

"What the fuck do they want to talk to us for?" Chrissy asked, breaking the silence.

"Well we're gonna find out soon kiddo. I've got a nasty feeling this is bigger than we think. I mean why outside our club?" The silence returned unbroken for nearly an hour as the two sat in deep thought until the doorbell announced the arrival of the police, making them both jump. Chrissy answered, not bothering to look through the little security hatch.

"Evening, officers," he said, pulling the door wide with a smile.

"You can take that smile off your fucking face Sonny we are here to investigate a murder not here for a fucking jolly!"

The senior detective barged through the door followed by his younger partner, both wearing knee-length rain coats and trilbies. Four uniformed constables followed in single file, all nodding as they passed Chrissy. Dixie was the last of them.

"Where's the boss?" the leading detective demanded over his shoulder.

"Just follow your nose, it's fucking big enough," Chrissy said under his breath barely hiding his contempt for the detectives.

Eddie rose from his chair, arm outstretched to shake the senior detective's hand. The detective halted in front of Eddie and looked him up and down for a few seconds. Eddie extended his arm. The policeman looked at it and huffed in disdain, ignoring the offer of the hand shake. He called over his shoulder to no- one in particular, "Search the place." The uniformed men sprang to life like so many bloodhounds, disappearing into various rooms, pulling boxes over, emptying out drawers and generally making a mess for the sake of it. The detective stood in front of Eddie, staring at him with a smug smile peeping out from under the bunch of greying hair on his top lip. He hated people like this. In his opinion the world had gone downhill since the war had finished. Bloody Irish and blacks streaming in to his beloved England, and now these jumped up Mods in their mohair suits and Italian shoes. The Teddy boys were bad enough in their ridiculous dress coats and quiffs but now he had to put up with these fucking immaculately dressed yobs flashing their money around; well, he'd show 'em, if there was no justice in the world then *he* would be the justice in Birmingham.

"Woah! Hold on! You're just meant to be here to ask questions, what the fuck do you think you're doing?" Chrissy had come in from the hall just as the chaos started. Eddie held his hand up to Chrissy gesturing him to be quiet and not to bother protesting. He knew this bastard was going to have his moment of power and enjoy it. "Don't worry Chrissy, they ain't gonna find nothing, we are a legit business."

The detective gave a little sarcastic laugh.

"So, that one's Christopher, and you must be Edward Fewtrell. Any relation to George Fewtrell?"

Chrissy spoke.

"That's our dad. What of it?" The policeman rocked back and forward on his feet, unable to contain his glee.

"Oh well I can see we are going to need to get more officers on the beat in this part of town now George's boys have come of age. If you're anything like your father, nothing's going to be safe unless it's screwed down."

Eddie ignored the jibe.

"And exactly how can we help you, officer?" he said staring him full in the face. The detective didn't answer. The two men stood silent, staring each other out. The younger detective spoke.

"Did either of you know the victim?" Eddie spoke, maintaining his stare,

"NO. There you are, that's that answered. Now you can go!" The older detective returned the look, letting the younger officer talk.

"Well, how can you say that when I haven't even told you his name yet?" The junior detective's words gave a sparkle to the older man's eyes.

Chrissy spoke up.

"How are we meant to know who it was?" His words hung in the air unanswered. "What is this, a fucking guessing game? Go on then, put us out of our misery, who was it?"

The older detective suddenly became animated.

"The body of the man found outside this very club was seen with your brother Christopher one week before he died." Chrissy looked perplexed. Eddie spoke up,

"He's a very popular lad. Between us we know hundreds of people.

Look, stop fucking around and tell us his name." The senior detective flinched at Eddie's words. "Mind your language when you talk to me or I'll . . . " Eddie finished off the sentence.

"Or you'll what. Either tell us his name or get the fuck out of my club."

The detective looked shocked. The younger officer had never seen the old man stuck for words before.

"You haven't got a search warrant, you haven't got a thing on us, otherwise you'd have nicked us already. Now stop fucking around and get off my property."

The old man raised his hand into a fist and made as if he was going to punch Eddie.

"I wouldn't do that, old fella." Chrissy spoke up. "It'll be the biggest mistake you'll ever make."

Hearing the confrontation, the uniformed officers began to gather back in the main bar expecting things to kick off, black truncheons in hand. There was a stand-off. The brothers stood side by side, backs against the bar, fists clenched with the policemen facing them in a semi-circle. The head detective stepped forward to make his move on Eddie. Then from the back of the room, a voice shouted out a name. "Micky Higgins!"

Everyone turned to see whose voice had interrupted the standoff.

"Micky Higgins," the voice said once more. "Micky Higgins. That's whose body we found outside."

Dixie stepped out of the office door into the bar area.

"Higgins?" repeated Chrissy. "Why would anyone kill Higgins?"

The older detective, now purple with rage, turned and marched over to Dixie.

"Just what the *fuck* do you think you're doing son? This is a *murder* investigation. *My* murder investigation and you're *inter-fuckingrupting* it!"

He spoke straight into the young constable's face nose to nose. Dixie pushed back with his forehead with just as much aggression. The two men broke away from each other.

"You're on fucking report, sonny!" blustered the old man.

"No sir, *you're* the one that's going on report. This isn't a murder investigation, this is harassment. I'll be taking this up with the chief when we get back to the station when I put in *my* report. We've got rules, you know."

Dixie replied, voice faltering slightly. Dixie knew his reply would create a shit storm from those above. But he also knew that the old man wasn't liked at the station and the chief had been very impressed with his latest case work. The Chiefs superintendent's voice played over their last conversation in Dixie's head.

"We will be looking for a new detective soon son as we are moving some of the older staff around, and if you carry on like this you'll reach great heights in the force. I've got great hopes for you, son." The memory of the Chief's inside information gave Dixie courage. The old man stood upright as if he'd received an electric shock, eyes wide, lips drawn tightly together.

"Just who the fuck do you think you're talking to, my lad?" The junior detective stepped forward glaring at Dixie but talking to his senior.

"Ehh sir, this is John Dix. He's the lad that solved the Jewellery Quarter robberies," he said hoping to calm the old man's reaction. But his words had the opposite effect. This sent the older detective into a blind rage. He had been in charge of that case too but hadn't been able to get anywhere with it due to the locals keeping their mouths shut. Then this Gloucester boy turns up and solves the case in *two weeks*.

"You think you can just waltz in to Birmingham, solve one crime, and suddenly you're Sherlock-fucking-Holmes. Then piss all over my murder investigation. You haven't got a clue have you, fucking country boy." The detective was spraying the words now, white spittle on the side of his mouth as he continued his rant.

"This city is full of vermin like these fucking Fewtrells and they need to be kept down where they belong in the gutters with all the other Birmingham rats!" His true thoughts were coming to the surface now. The other constables, all Birmingham born and bred, began to turn towards the detective.

"I've policed London, sonny. That's where the real crime is. Not here in this shit hole of an excuse for a city. That's where I should be with my talents, not here with these thick proletarian fuckers!" He gestured over his shoulder towards the uniformed officers who were starting to bristle at his words. "Now before your little interruption boy, I was going to teach these *legitimate businessmen* a lesson in how to talk to the law with respect."

He turned back towards the brothers who were still standing fists clenched and ready. "Right, you shower of arseholes, let's have 'em!" He stepped forward, expecting the uniformed men to join him in the beating he was about to lay out on the Fewtrell brothers. But the other policemen didn't move. His words had hit home. Up until then they hadn't realised how much contempt he held them in. If there was any beating to do, then he'd have to do it himself. They weren't about to beat up two Brummie lads for this Londoner with delusions of grandeur. He stepped forward without warning, throwing his fist towards Eddie, expecting to land a sucker punch on the young man's jaw. But Eddie saw it coming and moved his head to the side as the fist sailed past, spinning the old detective off balance. Eddie's fist flew up instinctively, reacting from years of boxing with his brothers. His fist caught the old man hard on the jaw. Eddie felt the bone break beneath the skin and the detective dropped to the floor, a dead weight, jaw broken. He lay motionless with his teeth protruding from his mouth at a weird angle, blood mixing with the spittle at the side of his mouth. The detective lay unconscious in his hospital bed for twenty four hours. With his jaw wired into place and unable to speak except for painful grunts he sat up in his bed staring at a report sheet, but for the life of him he couldn't remember what had happened. He remembered the body in the street and entering the club. Even talking in a heated manner to the owners. But after that it was a blur. A short visit from the chief superintendent had left him none the wiser, except for the fact that he was now to be transferred to a new branch called the city parks project. The chief had made it sound very exciting but the old man knew it was just lip service and his downward spiral within the force had now begun.

The junior detective and the uniformed men had all filled out their reports, all saying exactly same thing, about the interview with the Fewtrell brothers and how after the interview he had been drinking shots of whisky on the house, had lost his footing on the stairs to the office, falling and breaking his jaw in the process. What the report didn't say was how Eddie had taken control of the situation after the knockout had occurred, offering the junior detective and the constables drinks and a fairly large cash bribe if the incident didn't go further from the walls of the club. Dixie encouraged the other policemen to take the money, pointing out that the old detective was over the hill anyway and Eddie had done them all a favour. By the time the police went home they were legless drunk, lifetime members of the Bermuda club and fifty pounds each (*or* in old money, a month's wages) better off. Dixie had made a phone call to the station that they needed a Paddy wagon and an ambulance for the old man, and as the black police van pulled up off they went like some modern day keystone cops, carrying the old man by the arms and legs, his head hitting the floor as they stumbled out to the street. Eddie, Chrissy and Dixie stood in the doorway laughing at the spectacle.

The three men returned to the bar and talked until the early hours of what happened to Micky Higgins. The night was silent, only broken by the odd punter ringing the doorbell to the club every now and then trying to get a late night drink. Eddie insisted Chrissy tell him exactly what had taken place the last time he'd seen Higgins alive. Chrissy slowly opened up to them and the more he drank, the more detail came out.

"I ain't comfortable talking in front of no copper, however well you know him!" he said swigging a shot back. Eddie placed his hand on Dixie's shoulder.

"Don't worry about Dixie, he's one of us now; he's almost family. The higher we go, the higher he'll go if we work together. He's just proved himself hasn't he. There's one thing our Dad taught me," Eddie said addressing Chrissy, "If you can't beat 'em you've got to join 'em and we ain't gonna fucking beat 'em our kid. Look, ask yourself, why are we in this? I'll tell ya, to make fucking money and lots of it, yea?" he said, gesturing an open hand to Chrissy. Chrissy nodded back, agreeing and taking his brother's hand Eddie continued, "Well every other fucker in this town is trying to stop us making money. You know as well as I do there's people out there that'll slit your throat for a fiver. I mean, look what happened to poor Higgins for fuck's sake. We need to use the police to survive. Any tip of information or bit of muscle we can get, we need it, otherwise some other gang's gonna waltz in here and just take all our hard work away."

Dixie poured out more whisky into their glasses.

"Let me tell you, lads. That weren't no ordinary murder." They all looked at the policeman who by now had lost count of the whiskies he had drunk. "I didn't know your mate Higgins but whoever killed him enjoyed it, and no one deserves to die like he did."

The brothers turned their heads simultaneously towards Dixie.

"Go on!" Eddie said, his blue eyes wide in attention.

"Well . . . they cut bits off him." Dixie continued, hesitating as the images of what he'd seen replayed in his mind.

"What do you mean bits?" Eddie asked sternly. Dixie took another swig, grimacing against the strong whisky and the image burnt into his memory.

"All his fingers were gone and . . . and his bollocks had been cut off. We found them in his mouth for fuck's sake . . . but the worst thing was his face. It . . . was all distorted, frozen in agony. He must have suffered before he died, that poor kid. The whole thing gives me the creeps. Whoever did was a fucking psycho."

Dixie stopped suddenly, stood up raising his glass and made a toast,

"To business, family, and Micky Higgins."

They all stood, Chrissy swaying slightly. Eddie slapped Chrissy's back, smiling at him, and asked him yet again, "So carry on our kid, we need to know everything!"

Chrissy carried on telling them everything, only omitting the bit about Don's gun. As Chrissy talked, the rest of the brothers showed up at the club one by one.

Eddie introduced Dixie and filled them all in on what had been said about the events that had taken place. They all agreed that the Meat Market mob had just declared war on them but couldn't for the life of them work out why.

Frankie laughingly pointed out,

"This ain't because Eddie had shagged Toddy Burn's sister. Everyone's shagged Toddy Burn's sister, even Toddy." This broke the sombre mood and fresh drinks were poured around the bar.

"Ha, that's what I told him on the night," Chrissy laughed.

Dixie suggested that the best course of action was to wait and see what happened next. He would speak to his chief and see if he couldn't get some plain clothes officers to watch the market in case anything turned up.

"In the meantime," Eddie said, backing up Dixie's idea, "it's business as usual, eyes and ears open and gobs shut. Get it?" He finished firmly, "Let's see where this is going before we react."

The brothers agreed, and after some small talk they departed back to their homes the same way as they had arrived, until only Dixie and Eddie were left.

Eddie gave Dixie some information about a long-firming gang who were making it difficult for him to get his beer credit for the club.

The more the gang operated in the city the more the breweries were reluctant to give out credit on beer sales for fear of being ripped off. Eddie didn't see it as informing. As far as he was concerned if something affected his family in any way, then it was fair game. Dog eat dog.

Dixie left the club worse for wear in the first rays of the morning light, and went back to the station ready to break another case and take his next step up the ladder. Eddie laughed, "You're so pissed, you're more likely to break a fucking leg!" With that, the two men shook hands and parted.

Eddie shut the oak door smiling, but with a familiar empty feeling of dread in his gut. Somewhere in the back of his mind he knew that this was the start of another battle for survival for the Fewtrells. He couldn't tell from whom or where the fight was going to come, but he and his brothers had to be ready.

If he had the ability to see into the future, if he could have seen what was coming down the line at him over the next few months, maybe he would've locked the door to the Bermuda club for good and walked away into the purple light of the new day forever.

Plans are Drawn

Chapter 5

Reggie was very pleased with himself. Not only had he held the meeting on his own without his brother Ronnie, but he had also secured a deal with the Americans that could get them out of the extortion business and into a much more profitable one, without any of the hassle from the other London gangs.

The Americans had done their best to impress and it had worked. A baby blue Chevrolet with a fawn leather interior had pulled up outside their mom's house, and the whole street came out to see who it was. Film stars, politicians; the murmur had gone around the streets of the East End until there were nearly a hundred or so people outside the house clamouring for a glimpse at a real life American.

Four men stepped out of the car, all suntanned and in shining, gailycoloured mohair suits in pastel shades. Reggie peered through the net curtains at the car outside.

"Leave 'em to stew for a few minutes," he said to the two firmmen standing by his shoulders. After ten minutes had passed, Reggie stepped out onto the street and greeted them in his usual black three button and black tie, feeling like an undertaker compared to the four yanks.

"Hello mate," he said, smiling, "I'm Reg, welcome to the East End." With that, a cheer went up from the crowd. The yanks looked pleasantly surprised by the welcome. Little Nicky Scarfo, head of the Atlantic City mob, turned to Reggie smiling,

"Did you guys put this on just for us?" he said, waving regally at the gathering crowd. Reggie laughed.

"No mate they think you're a facking movie star. They ain't never seen a real American before."

The two men turned and gave the crowd a wave.

"Come on inside lads, I'll get me Mam to put the kettle on and we'll 'av a cuppa tea."

The Americans followed Reggie into the small terraced house that belonged to their mother, a safe house where the Kray brothers always held their meetings.

The house was hallowed ground, a place where they grew up and felt comfortable. The cheerful little front room of the house had a large oval dark wood dining table with eight chairs around it. The little Victorian fire place crackled, warming the room. Along the wall under the window was one of Ronnie's vivariums. Inside, curled around a small log, lay a large yellow and white snake. The Yanks seemed very impressed by the exotic creature, especially little Nicky.

"What da fuck! Hey Reggie, is this what ya feed your fucking enemies to? I gotta get me one of these fucking things," he chuckled, "with all *my* enemies it'd be as fat as my fucking wife!" The men burst into laughter as they took their seats around the table. Right on cue, Mrs Kray came in with a large pot of tea and various cakes on a silver tray she saved for best. Reggie introduced her to the four Americans and after a little small talk she left. Little Nicky pointed to the empty chair where Ronnie usually sat.

"Where's your brother? I was told that you two were inseparable."

Reggie was wondering the same thing. Ronnie hadn't said he wasn't coming, but his driver had mentioned to Reggie that he was taking Ronnie to a special party in the West end somewhere, so Reggie assumed that Ronnie was sleeping off a hangover.

In truth, Reggie was relieved his brother wasn't there. Lately Ronnie's mood swings had become very aggressive, with the slightest thing starting them off. The last two meetings with other friendly London gangs had been ruined by his distorted grasp of reality, driving what were once Kray-friendly gangs into their enemies' hands.

"I'm afraid we'll have to start without him. He ain't very well." Reggie said, lying.

"Nothing serious I hope?" Nicky replied, pretending to care. "No, Ronnie is as ard as nails. He's just feeling under the weather and didn't want to give you all the flu by being ere. He's gutted though, and sends his compliments."

The Americans started the meeting with a gift.

"I would like to present this token from myself and our partners in New York whom I represent, as a small token of our respect." Little Nicky gestured to his associate who then stepped forward with a small black box handing it to Reggie. Reggie took the box and, smiling, opened it to reveal a small solid silver Statue of Liberty figurine inside.

"Thank you gentlemen, our mother will love it," he said grinning. He nodded to the man on his shoulder who in turn passed Reggie a long beautifully engraved samurai sword. Reggie held the sword in two hands and lay it on the table in front of Nicky.

"It's a genuine 15th century sword from Japan. My brother and I would like you to have it, Mr Scarfo."

Little Nicky was genuinely surprised. He picked the sword up and pulled the blade from its sheath. The gleaming steel on its razor sharp blade reflected the smile on his face. He placed the sword back on the table and stood up. Walking around the oval table to where Reggie stood he grabbed him with both hands on the shoulders and kissed him once on each cheek.

"Mr Kray," he said, true emotion in his voice, "that is the greatest gift anyone has ever given me. A sword from a warrior, to a warrior." Slapping Reggie's shoulders, he returned to his chair.

"Wow, wait till I get back to Atlantic City; there's gonna be some fucking heads rolling then I can tell ya!" The men began laughing again.

"Now then, my English friend, let's get down to the business at hand."

The two men talked for hours. Little Nicky Scarfo and the New York mobsters were looking at introducing and supplying London with grade A heroin. The drug had done very well for them on the East coast and West coast of America and now they were making a push at Europe. They said it was the modern drug and once tried people were hooked for good. The Kray twins had come to the attention of the mob, so they were to be given first refusal. Reggie knew that a refusal to deal with the Yanks wasn't an option, because if he did the Americans would simply go elsewhere and the Krays weren't the only gang around London who could handle this.

But that wasn't the only reason. If the brothers didn't want the deal on the table, then the New York mob would make sure that they didn't get anything from anyone's table by turning the other gangs against them. Over the past few months they had already started hearing disrespectful comments about Ronnie's private life from other gang members, and word was spreading that they were just a couple of flash in the pan queers, on the make.

This didn't sit well with Reggie. He wasn't a queer and hated the suggestion that he was. So this was a chance to re-establish the Firm as a force to be reckoned with. Of course it would mean they would have to expand into other areas but they could sort the details out when Ronnie arrived and the Yanks had left.

The Americans had sorted out how they were going to bring it into England; all the Krays had to do was set up a distribution network, and they were in business. There was plenty of room for movement on price too and that was without even taking into account that the twins intended to cut the heroin with other substances to increase their profits by another third.

This would be a perfect sideline business to run alongside the clubs and protection rackets. But Reggie didn't savour the idea of telling Ronnie what he had agreed to. He wasn't scared. He just knew that Ronnie would take his lone decision as a personal paranoid attack on their partnership.

Two days passed before Ronnie resurfaced. The speed he had taken at Lord Boothby's party had worn off and with the help of the valium and a couple of sharp whiskies and he had slept like the dead for nearly a whole twenty four hours. His amphetamine come-down hung over him like a shadow and Ronnie couldn't face anyone or anything, shutting himself away in his apartment, drifting in and out of his sleepy depression.

The loud ring of a phone broke his sanctity at 8am. Reggie was on the other end of the phone. He was worried, and said they needed to talk. He said something about meeting at the Blind Beggar, Whitechapel at midday. Ronnie hung up without saying if he'd be there or not.

The Blind Beggar has been a drinking establishment in one form or another for hundreds of years. The walls had changed from wattle and daub to brick, but it's foundations had seen the comings and goings of Kings and Queens, dictators and democrats. Now these new self-appointed lords of London, the Krays, occupied the building as a meeting place for their gang. In historic terms they were just a couple of newcomers but they were just as violent and self-obsessed as anyone that had trodden a path through Whitechapel in the past five hundred years.

Ronnie stepped out of the gleaming grey Jaguar on to the pavement like a young prince. His grey, mohair suit shined like modern-day chain mail.

Reggie watched from inside the pub, the sight of his twin calming his mood. Ronnie was pissed off about something or other, he could see that. He wasn't looking forward to telling him about his meeting with Yanks.

Ronnie had a newspaper in his hands and was staring at it, brow furrowed, as if something in it had caught his attention, sending him into a trance. After a few seconds he rolled the paper under his arm and stepped inside the pub. The various members of the Firm who were scattered about the pub having drinks suddenly stopped their conversations as Ronnie entered. His aura filled the pub instantly, creating a feeling of being in the room with a mad dog that could snap out at anyone at any time. Some of the men shrank deeper into pretend conversations, hoping they wouldn't be noticed. The older, harder more established of the men bade him good morning. Ronnie knew what they thought of him and he loved it. He wanted them to be scared. He encouraged it. Fear was as sign of respect and they feared him. He looked at no-one and strode on through the room to the back bar which acted as their unofficial office.

"The usual, darlin'," he said across the bar to the star-struck barmaid. He pushed the partition doors open to see Reggie for the first time in days. Reggie rose from the table, hand extended, smiling. Ronnie ignored him, slamming the newspaper down onto the table.

"What is this facking country coming to?" He stood pointing at the headlines, eyes glaring. Reggie sat back onto the red leather bench sighing. He picked up the paper. *Boy's body found in the Thames.* "Facking disgrace."

Ronnie couldn't bring himself to look at the picture of the small blonde haired blue eyed boy on the front page. Reggie looked perplexed.

"What the fack's this got to do with us, Ron? This type of thing's been happening in London for years. Some pervert's had his way with the lad ain't he?" Ronnie flinched at the words, picturing the man hitting the child by the fireplace two nights before.

He ran through the night's events. Maybe he could have done more to help the kid, taken him under his wing, saved him. But in the back of his mind he knew that the boy was just another sacrifice to London. Another soul given to the gods of wealth, power and perversion in the most corrupt city the world had seen since the glory days of Rome. He had justified many souls like this and the boy's wouldn't be the last. Ronnie's mood swung into a lighter shade as his drink arrived at the table.

"All I'm saying is it's a facking shame. Handsome kid, bladdy shame." Reggie nodded.

"Yea, he's like a young Lawrence of Arabia ain't he?" He held the paper up to Ronnie showing the picture taken when the boy still had his whole life ahead of him.

"You mean Peter O'Toole!" Ronnie said laughing, shying away from the black and white photo.

Reggie asked, "Did you know the kid?"

Ronnie took a sip from his drink.

"Nah." Reggie didn't need to ask any more. He knew from his brother's reaction that he was involved somehow, but didn't press him further. Changing the subject, he smiled,

"Can we talk some business now bruv?" He said smiling, "I've got a bit of news about the Yanks."

They talked face to face deeply about the proposition the Americans had offered. At first Ronnie wasn't keen, pointing out the film and TV stars they were hanging out with now. Drugs were dirty, below them. They had a standard to keep up now. They were celebrities in their own right.

Reggie agreed that they would have to keep their distance from the dealing side of things, but in return he pointed out that their grip on much of the territory they had fought for with the other London gangs was being eroded.

"We need this deal. The money it'll generate will put everything else into shadow. Besides, there's no glory in roughing up club owners for a few quid any more. We gotta think bigger."

Reggie almost pleaded with his brother. "Anyway, if we don't do it the Yanks will just go to someone else and then we'll have another load of shit on our plate."

"True, Reg, true."

Ronnie sat fingering the top of his glass. "How about this. How about we don't do it in London to start with. What about we start somewhere else?" Reggie looked confused. "Somewhere like Brighton?"

"No not facking Brighton, it's full of poofs!" Reggie realised what he'd said. "No offence bruv." "None taken." Ronnie scowled.

"Look, we already got the biggest city in Britain. How about we start it in the second biggest city in Britain." Ronnie began to get excited at his own idea.

"Where the fack's that then?" Reggie asked, hands flat on the table.

They both sat there in silence, neither of them knowing the answer to the question. Ronnie was convinced it was Newcastle, he had contacts there and was starting to insist that they start there. Reggie wasn't so sure and decided to get other opinions. He rose from the table and went through to the other bar.

"Anyone know what Britain's second city is?" Many of them men looked non plussed but one man held his hand up, as if he were in a school lesson, smiling sheepishly. His name was Freddy Finger, a young ginger lad in his early twenties, so called as he seemed to have a finger in every pie in London, and he was about get his dirty little mincers into one more.

"Well, . . . It's facking Birmingham ain't it Boss?" he said, embarrassed that the Krays didn't know the answer to such a simple question.

"Tell me more Freddy." Reggie patted Freddy Finger on the shoulder, gloating at his brother who had now followed him in to the bar.

"Well it's Britain's second city. About a million people, it's only an hour and a half away if you put your foot down. I was up there last week with Freddy Foreman and some of the lads, we were on the piss. Theres a club called the Elbow Room, a lot of the London lads drink there, it's a great laugh." Freddy had started to grow in the Kray's spotlight. "There's trains that go there direct from Victoria station too." Reggie had lost interest by the time Freddy had finished his sentence. He walked back through to the pub lounge with his brother.

"Birmingham . . . it's perfect . . . We could send the courier up on a facking train. That's where we'll start it. Easy to get to, so supply will be no problem and plenty of people to sell to. We won't be connected to it and those Northern fackers won't know what's hit 'em. We might be able to muscle in on a few clubs along the way. It's a facking good idea Ron."

Ronnie smiled and held his glass up. "So I take it we're doing it then."

"Facking right." Reg countered.

"Of course, "Ronnie said, having one of his rare cautious moments, "we'll have to go and give the place a look over. Meet some of the locals, get 'em on side so to speak."

"And if they won't come onside?" Reggie grinned.

"Divide and conquer. We'll turn one lot against the other. It's always worked in the past and it'll work again. We don't need to get our hands dirty any more. We're above all that shit now. Even if it is fun." Ronnie was enjoying the sound of his own voice.

The brothers clinked glasses and the deal was done. Reggie was relieved that his brother had taken it on board so quickly.

"Who do we know from Birmingham?"

"I dunno anyone." they were silent once more until Reggie called for Freddy Finger to come into the lounge. The brothers pressed him for a contact.

"Well . . . There's a few blokes from there knocking around, but they're all small time. There is this one bloke that springs to mind though; Tom Shellby. He used to have a gang there years ago called Peaky Blinders. He did very well on the horses apparently. I don't know him personally but I know people that know him, if you know what I mean."

Reggie wanted to know if he could be trusted, how he made his money and the like. Freddy Finger had started to enjoy this attention, becoming more confident with his answers.

"Well Reg, he's well known for fixing races, horses and dogs, but mainly the gee gees. He's been at it for years. He runs a racket at the Warwick races . . . that's only down the road from Birmingham. If anyone knows about Birmingham, it'll be him."

Ronnie called across the bar to the young dark haired girl polishing glasses, "Tell 'em they can come in now."

She disappeared and a low murmur came from the other bar, and slowly the hard men of the Firm came through the stained glass partition doors. Freddy sat between the twins smiling at his associates as they entered the room, pleased with his new celebrity.

"Hello lads!" Reggie said, rising from the bench. "Anyone know a bloke called Tom Shellby? We're all going on a bit of an adventure up north and we need his help."

The men looked around at each other. One of them stepped forward.

Pat Connelly, one of the most loyal of the Kray's Firm, spoke up.

"I know someone that knows him. He's a bookie down the West End. He's mentioned him loads of times." Ronnie took the lead now.

"Nice one Pat. Well go and *ask* Mr Shellby if he would like our invitation to dinner tonight at the Double R club as our guest. Tell him all we want is some information about Birmingham." Reggie stepped forward.

"Yea, nothing to worry about. Make sure you tell him that too. We don't want scare him."

With that Pat Connelly turned and pointed at two of the other men, who both followed him onto the street.

Ronnie raised his glass to the girl behind the bar.

"Two more G&Ts darlin', and get this lot what they want too. We're facking celebrating!"

Ronnie waited until everyone had a glass. "Gentlemen, to expansion!"

The men raised their glasses to each other and drank as if the outcome of the adventure was already a forgone conclusion.

Ronnie's mind was on their plan now: Americans, Birmingham, heroin, money and expansion.

The image of the blue eyed blonde haired boy was long forgotten. Greed was a far more comfortable emotion than empathy.

Stirring the Nest

Chapter 6

"What the fuck were you thinking?" Toddy Burns slammed his fist on the table sending beer glasses jumping in the air. "I told you we would deal with it in time. Not fucking . . . *this*!"

He threw a newspaper across the table into Jarvis's face. Jarvis picked the paper up from where it fell and rearranged the pages. The front page had a large black and white photo on it. A young man's body, shown in all its gruesome detail, lay in a strange posture on a road with headlines saying *Tortured to Death.* Jarvis looked over the picture and took in every inch of it. A smirk grew on his face, as the memories of how the man had ended up like he appeared in the photo ran through his mind. Jarvis turned his face towards the window savouring the thoughts. Without looking at Toddy he folded the paper and put it inside his coat.

"He had it coming Toddy." His voice sounded like a scolded child, with no real conviction in his words. "Killed two birds with one stone so to speak . . . excuse the pun."

He gave a little laugh hoping to lighten Toddy's mood. Toddy looked shocked.

"Killed . . . killed is one thing this is . . . fucking sick. Do you get a kick out of this or something? I mean . . . I'm struggling here, Jarvis, I'm trying to understand what fucking possessed you to slaughter Micky fucking Higgins. I know his dad for fuck's sake. He buys from the market. People are gonna talk. Besides he wasn't anything to do with the fucking Fewtrells."

Jarvis turned back to face Toddy, his confidence growing.

"He was one of 'em. Make no mistake about that. I did us all a favour. Anyway the coppers will be all over this by now. It sent a message not to fuck with us. Toddy, we gotta show strength."

Toddy leant forward across the table staring deep into the other man's eyes.

"I don't think you've grasped the situation, mate. I was just gonna smash up their club send 'em a message about who runs this city, *not* start a fucking war. The police won't give a fuck about some Irish kid getting himself killed. But a murder is a murder and soon they'll start taking a look around at everyone and anyone and I don't want some copper poking his nose in my business. We got a good screw going on here. Last thing we need is unwanted attention."

Jarvis picked his drink from the table and gave a sigh. He sat crossed legged and effeminate under Toddy's gaze.

"That's why I did it. To draw attention from us and onto them." He sounded almost tearful.

"There was no attention on us!" Toddy screamed. "Killing Micky Higgins is gonna bring a lot of attention on us now though, you fucking idiot!"

Jarvis had never seen Toddy so angry.

"You and your queer mates had better sort this out. Cos I ain't looking over my shoulder, waiting for one of the Fewtrells to shoot me in the back for the rest of my life." Jarvis looked confused.

"And if the old Bill come sniffing, you don't know anything. Understand? Fucking nothing."

The two men sat in silence for a while, each lost in his own thoughts. The noise of the buses loading their passengers outside the window of the Market Tavern was the only sound in the empty bar. The damp smell of last night's beer in the carpet hung in the air compounding the feeling of dread hanging over the men. Toddy spoke first. "I'm gonna go and tell the boys in the Mob that we had nothing to do with any of this and your just gonna *mention* that you think the Fewtrells did it. You're not gonna tell 'em anymore than that, no details, just a suspicion. That's all we're gonna do. Let them think things up for themselves. Then when the police come around, one of the lads will let it slip accidentally and the heat will be off of us. Not only that but we'll be creating a bit of hatred towards the Fewtrells, and when the time comes to strike they'll have a cause to get behind. We'll be seen to stand by Micky Higgins' family too. Start a collection for the funeral costs, that type of thing. I'll turn this situation in our favour, and save us from this fuck up you've created."

Toddy stood up and walked away without looking at Jarvis. He felt reborn. The panic had gone now. He had a plan and needed to get things moving. His first call was to give his condolences to Mr & Mrs Higgins.

The door slammed behind him as he left the pub.

Jarvis sat alone in the dank bar, smoking and drinking his way through the *Babycham* he'd helped himself to from behind the bar. He wasn't worried about Toddy's anger. He could see the big man was just scared.

"If Toddy Burns thinks I'm gonna stop now, just when things are geting lively, he's got another thing coming," he thought to himself.

He pulled the newspaper from his pocket and looked over the picture again. As Jarvis's eyes ran across the page he began to get a familiar tingling inside. He looked around the room, making sure no-one could see him from the street outside, and when he had assured himself he was alone, he undid the belt on his trousers and slid them to the floor. He slid his hand inside his underwear and began feeling himself, all the time his stare unbroken at the picture. Only in his mind he didn't see the face of the young Irishman he had destroyed. He saw Chrissy Fewtrell bound and gagged instead. Caught up in the sadistic fantasy playing in his mind, he continued to pleasure himself in the darkened empty bar just out of sight from the buses and pedestrians passing by only inches away through the pub windows.

The Cedar Club

Chapter 7

Hazel Fewtrell stood in the red phone box, shifting her weight from one foot to the other excitedly. Eddie waited outside, hands dug into the pockets of his coat, watching out for parking attendants, more interested in his Ford Consul than anything Hazel was up to. She hung up the phone smiling, and stepped out into the cold breeze.

"We're gonna see it this afternoon," she said giggling.

She had been trying to encourage Eddie to open a legitimate club for some time now, and the man on the other end of the phone had tipped her off about an empty warehouse that he thought would fit the bill. Until this point, Eddie had been humouring her, but now he was genuinely interested in Hazel's little project.

If Eddie was the muscle in the relationship, then Hazel was the brains. Eddie had always had a hard time shaking off the market boy wheeler and dealer persona. Make no mistake, Eddie was a sharp thinker as well a good fighter. But Hazel had the foresight to be able to see that the Bermuda club was just a stop gap until they opened a real club and although slight, she could throw a good punch too.

Hazel had plans for Eddie and herself. She had been to London and seen the future, and she wanted some of it.

Birmingham didn't have any real town centre clubs. No one was bringing in the big acts that were touring the country yet. Yes, there were various venues around the city that put on bands. But it was only a matter of time before someone caught on to the idea of a real city centre night club, and she was going to make sure that the Fewtrells got there first.

Their courtship had been a messy affair with plenty of beatings being handed out to various other suitors by Eddie and his brothers. But in the end he won her over with his manic charisma and never-ending promises. Born in Aston, her dark Italian looks disguised her Irish Liverpool roots. She had a sophisticated aura that belied her pauper background. With the lack of a mother in the family, the younger Fewtrell boys gave her the respect she demanded and she repaid it with her loving nature. As she integrated herself into the Fewtrell family life she became a wing for the younger brothers to shelter under when the elder boys got out of hand, and a filter for any of the would-be girlfriends who had began to smell success, floating in and out of their lives like so much flotsam and jetsam. The cold rain fell for Micky Higgins across the grey city.

His funeral had been organised very quickly, and caught many people by surprise. It was unusual to have a funeral on a Friday.

Eddie and Hazel had got wind of it the day it was being held and had visited the Higgins household beforehand to pay their respects. But their visit had been frosty to say the least with Micky's mother openly blaming the Fewtrells for her son's death. Eddie had tried to give his father some money towards the funeral costs, but was told in no uncertain terms that they didn't need it and "Micky's *real* friends at the market have already paid for everything." Eddie told them that neither he nor any of his brothers had anything to do with Micky's death, and that Micky was a good friend. But his protest had the opposite effect, with the mother breaking down in tears and the father virtually throwing them out of the house. Meekly, they drove back into the town centre with not a word spoken between the two until they pulled up outside the empty warehouse they had arranged to look over for the new club.

Eddie felt angry about the confrontation, but Hazel's feelings bordered more on shame.

Eddie had promised her that he had nothing to do with Micky's death but in reality she really couldn't spot the difference between Eddie's version of the truth, the real truth or a lie. Eddie's manic behaviour seemed to cloak his real intentions and Hazel had yet to find a way to decipher it.

They decided there and then not to attend the funeral. The last thing they needed would be a confrontation with the meat market mob at a funeral for their friend. The papers might even be there, and if Hazel's plans for a new club went ahead they would have to distance themselves as far as possible from Micky's murder.

The estate agent was standing in the shadows in a doorway on the old Constitution Hill. The building didn't look like much, but as they stepped through the doors into what was once a warehouse, Eddie and Hazel's minds began to soar.

The couple started to point out to each other what would go where.

"The stage is here, and the dance floor, there." Eddie barked. "No!" Hazel disagreed. "If we knock down this wall and look at the room long ways we'll get more people in and the bar can run along that wall over there." Eddie nodded, unable to think of a better solution but peeved that Hazel had thought of it and not him.

The arguments went on as they wandered the labyrinth of rooms. But they knew right from the start that this was going to be something big. After a few hours of arranging and rearranging the rooms in their minds, Eddie shook the agent's hand and a deal was struck.

"I want the first six months rent free." Eddie said in his best businessman voice. "Give us time to fix the place up."

The agent looked at them both across the top of his silver rimmed glasses as if he had smelled something rotten.

"Mr Fewtrell, this is a prime location. There are other people who are after this space and I can assure you it won't hang around too long. There won't be any deals on the rent. This isn't the Rag market you know."

Eddie wasn't sure if the estate agent had ever known that he had worked in the rag market or not, but he had worked hard to pull himself and his family out of the gutter, and any reference to the Fewtrell's humble backgrounds was definitely the wrong thing to say. Eddie stepped forward and grabbed the agent's jacket lapels.

"I ain't making any fucking deals. I ain't asking for six months off the rent. I'm telling you that's what's gonna happen. Do you understand, you fucking ponce!" Eddie pulled the tall skinny man towards his face. The estate agent's eyes widened, and his mouth began to put together words, but just wouldn't form a sentence until he muttered,

"I'll . . . I'll call the police!"

Eddie held him tight by the lapels and shook him.

"Call the fucking police then. Go on, I'll drive you to the fucking phone box if you like. You think I'm scared of the fucking police, you dirty ponce?"

The agent dropped his briefcase, papers falling all over the floor. Hazel could see the man's eyes starting to roll in his head, and she thought he might pass out altogether.

"Leave him alone, you bloody big ape," she said, a look of false concern on her face.

She stepped between the two, forcing a gap and bringing a stop to the roughing up of the old gentleman.

"Do you always have to be so aggressive? You and your bloody eight brothers," she said, looking at Eddie with a glint in her eye. "Oh, I'm so sorry about my husband. He's very forceful. He has to be, otherwise he wouldn't be leader of his gang you see."

The agent's eyes began to focus on her now. Hazel dropped her voice to a whisper.

"If I were you I'd do as he says. My husband's a bloody lunatic, and he's the calm one in the gang. Some of his brothers would just slit your throat just for saying you're going to police. You see, the problem you've got is that even if you report Eddie to the Old Bill, one of his brothers will get you."

Hazel paused to see if her words were getting through to the old man. His look of terror confirmed that her warning was beginning to sink in, and the agent was coming to terms with the choice of either getting a good hiding or six months rent free to the young hoodlum. He decided to go with the latter.

Eddie beamed, his persona changing instantly

"Thanks pal. I'll get my brief to sort the paperwork out with ya."

The door to the empty warehouse slammed shut as the couple made their exit. The old man sat for a few minutes on the dusty floor in silence. His heart was pounding against his tweed waistcoat as he drew himself up to gather the fallen paperwork. He didn't realise it at the time, but he had just made one of the best deals of his life.

Black and Tans

Chapter 8

The thought had never dawned on Toddy Burns, as he carried the coffin of Micky Higgins through the wet streets to the awaiting hearse, that the man inside the box would still have been alive if he had just allowed Chrissy Fewtrell to buy some bacon and eggs.

The triviality of the cause of Micky's torturous death was none of his concern. All Toddy was thinking about was getting to the pub after the graveside to give Micky a good send off in the Irish style as his family wanted it. He had arranged everything for them; food, drinks, even Irish musicians to liven things up a bit.

The irony of having Toddy Burns, Duncan Jarvis and the rest of the people responsible for their son's passing to carry their son's coffin to the graveside was lost on his parents.

The graveyard was an old Victorian slab of land on the outskirts of town in an area called Hockley. The old grave stones had turned black in the torrential rain, and the whole area had the feeling of decay and oppression. This was amplified by the small groups of darkly dressed Mob members scattered around the graves keeping watch for any Fewtrells who might turn up to pay their respects. The rain continued to fall as the Meat Market Mob lowered the dark wood box into its final resting place. Toddy stood opposite Jarvis as they held onto the strops holding the coffin as it sank into the wet cold earth. He thought he saw a small smirk grow on Jarvis' lips, sending the tiniest of shivers down his spine, as he came to terms with the monster he had befriended.

But he blamed the shiver he felt as cold on his bones. He was unwilling and unable to accept any responsibility for any of the events of the past few weeks, preferring instead to lay the blame firmly on Eddie Fewtrell and the rest of his clan.

Micky's wake was a riot to say the least. The turn-out at the graveside had been poor due to the mixture of Micky's youth, driving rain and the speed in which the funeral had been organised. But if the graveyard had a lack of willing souls to mourn his death his wake; on the other hand, hundreds had shown up to celebrate his life over a drink or several.

It seemed that most of the huge Irish community was trying to cram into the back room of the Irish centre in Digbeth. After a short time, the room was at bursting point and Toddy had to have the doors opened into the main hall. The people spilled out, filling the tables and filling the main hall straight away. Even the Birmingham Irish pipe and drums had shown up in their smart dark green jackets with gleaming silver harp-shaped buttons, saffron kilts and caubeens. Also, a large part of the Jamaican Caribbean community had turned up. The Meat Market Mob boys who attended were shocked at the jollity of the event. Even Micky's mother and father were on the dance floor, kicking their heels as the band played the *Siege of Ennis.* As the beer flowed, so did more and more of the Irish of Birmingham into the hall.

Toddy was drunk and had noisily gathered the mob around him about to explain how they were going to smash the Bermuda club and drive the Fewtrells back to Aston.

His boys nodded and made brash comments about kicking in heads and breaking noses and the like, as young drunken men tend to do. Just as Toddy was in full swing they were interrupted by several Irish men with serious expressions on their faces.

"Let me tell ye boys, the Fewtrells didn't have a hand in this. Not their style."

Toddy turned towards the voice.

"No, if Eddie Fewtrell wanted ye dead, he'd just make ye disappear.

None of this torture bull-shite"

The blond Irishman with a scar down his left cheek clicked his fingers. "Disappear, just like that, so he would."

Toddy slammed his glass down on the bar, the boys from the mob doing the same.

"Oh, really? And who the fuck says so?"

The Irishman smirked, "Who says so, ye say?" The group of Irish gathered around their spokesman. "The fecking IRA says so, that's who."

He almost shouted the words above the music. People around the bar stopped drinking and started to take notice. Toddy went white in the face, realising that this could turn nasty as he suspected everyone in the hall was an IRA sympathiser and would like nothing more than giving some English boys a good kicking.

"Well we ain't got no argument with the IRA have we lads?" His bravado had gone, and the lads from the mob were shuffling about like so many scolded school boys, nodding their heads. For the life of him, Toddy couldn't work out what the connection was between the Irish and the Fewtrells. "But let me tell you mate," he retorted with as much backbone as possible, "the Fewtrells did this, no doubt about it."

The Irishman stepped forward straight into Toddy's face.

"No lad, this was someone trying to make a point. Trying to send a signal. The police might fall for it but we know better, don't we lads." The men who stood behind the large Irishman all nodded as well as some of the people surrounding the circle of men who were eavesdropping.

"Ai. If Eddie had done it we would've been informed." said one of the group.

"You see, Micky Higgins was one of ours and we know that Eddie, Chrissy or any of the Whizz Mob for that matter wouldn't be involved in this."

He looked around for assurance from the growing group of IRA men. A thick Belfast accent spoke up from inside the circle.

"There's no way on God's green earth any of the Fewtrells would have crossed the IRA by killing young Higgins. No-fecking-way!" Toddy could feel the blood drain from his face and a cold sweat climbed up his back.

"Which brings me to my next point, boyo," the Irishman continued, "Micky's mother and father told us how you so kindly paid and arranged for all of this." He swept his hand around the room. "Tell me, Mr Burns, why? You and your pals here don't strike me as people that are overly fond of the Irish. It's a well-known fact that you and your boys keep the Irish from trading in the market. So why are you bending over backwards to help the Higgins family?"

The cold sweat had risen from Toddy's back to his forehead now. He opened his mouth to talk but Jarvis stepped in front of him. "It was me, mate. I'm Irish Catholic from Liverpool and I made 'em do it."

The big Irishman looked Jarvis up and down.

"Micky was a mate and I just thought we should show solidarity with his family is all," Jarvis said, his voice wavering slightly. The Irishman was visibly disgusted at the high-pitched effeminate voice of the wiry red quaffed Scouser stood in front of him.

Without warning, the IRA man slapped Jarvis around the face with such force it nearly knocked him off his feet. Both groups of men prickled ready to fight.

"I talk to the grinder not his fecking monkey."

He raised his hand towards the exit.

"Well, Mr Burns, it's been nice chatting, but if I were you I'd leave right now, before we show you what we really think of you British bastards." The blonde Irishman looked straight at Jarvis whilst addressing Toddy. "And take that . . . thing with you."

Toddy had poured his beer from his glass jug and held it by the handle in case it all kicked off.

"Come on lads," he said calmly. "Obviously we're not wanted here." He could see that his boys were ready to fight, but a short glance around the room made it very clear they were well outnumbered and although they could put up a good fight there was no way they could win.

Toddy began to back out of the main entrance to the hall, leading to the side-street outside. His mob gathered around him. Jarvis had led the way out onto the street, followed by the rest of his associates, and then at the rear were the growing group of Irish who gathered in the doorway watching the Meat Market Mob back off across the road. Jarvis reached the other side of the road and, without turning, he shouted over his shoulder,

"Why don't you fuck off back to Ireland, you thick Paddy cunts?" His words were greeted by sniggers from his gang mates.

"Yea fuck off, Paddy or we'll send in the Black and Tans again." Toddy joined in. But the Irish didn't hear Toddy's words as they had started singing an Irish rebel song.

"*Oh come out you Black and Tans*!" They sang in unison, strong and proud.

"*Come out and fight me like a man,*" knowing that the words would sting the British boys as they retreated up the main street back to the town centre.

"*And how the IRA made you run like hell away.*" The words to the song carried along the deserted road, bouncing off the grey concrete buildings, amplifying the meaning and driving the insult home.

The gang marched back to what they considered their headquarters, the Market Tavern. The streets were empty as the cold drizzle fell softly in the twilight of the early evening, making the dirty streets seem clean and new. The place was empty and about to shut even though it was only seven pm due to the out of business opening times. But Toddy convinced the landlord to leave the keys and the gang set about the bar. Beer and shorts were poured out for all and the banter started in earnest, mainly Anti-Irish rhetoric, but Toddy kept bringing the subject back to the Fewtrells, laying the blame for everything firmly at their door.

Even though they thought it, no-one amongst group mentioned Micky Higgins' connection to the IRA, or what the Irishman had said about the Fewtrells not being involved. The more alcohol they consumed, the louder and more defiant they got.

"We should go up the Bermuda club and batter them fuckers right now," Toddy shouted. The other men nodded and yelled their support.

"What about the Irish? If we batter the Fewtrells, the IRA might get involved," one of the younger men pointed out.

"Fuck the IRA. They ain't gonna blow the meat market up are they? Anyway, the Fewtrells open their doors to fucking anyone. Irish, blacks, even fucking gypos. They need bringing down a fucking peg or two. I say let's head up there and batter 'em. Who's with me?" The Mob acted as one, jumping to their feet, fists in the air.

"Right, let's have a few more drinks. I'll get on the phone and get some more bodies here. Then we'll head up to the Bermuda and fucking wreck the place. Put 'em out of business, lads!"

A loud cheer went up, and the drinking began again. Only Jarvis stayed quiet. He had stuck his neck out for Toddy once more and got slapped and humiliated for his trouble. He wasn't in the mood for big talk. He wanted something a little bit more real. Flesh and blood. Something he could get his teeth into. Without saying goodbye, he headed out of the front door towards the Trocadero to release the tension and claim his pound of flesh.

New Kingdom

Chapter 9

Ron and Reg couldn't believe how short the trip to Birmingham was. Between chatting and planning their city takeover the journey had just flown by. The gunmetal grey Jaguar purred along the motorway until Birmingham city centre came into view. Both of the brothers were impressed by how modern the city looked, were as London was old and rough and spread out Birmingham was compact and exciting. Buildings like the Rotunda and The Bull Ring looked like something from the future which gave them both a good feeling about the place. They parked at the Holiday Inn and Tom Shellby's man was waiting there for them as arranged. After a short introduction and hand shake they retired to their rooms to freshen up. Ronnie waited for Reggie to go ahead and pulled Shellby's man to one side.

"Ear mate. Where do the . . . *actors* drink in this town?" The man didn't really understand the question but guessed at its meaning. He told him all he knew about the Trocadero which wasn't much but Ronnie had all the information he needed. Nodding he disappeared into the lift to smarten up for the night's adventures. Two hours later both brothers appeared in smart black suits looking pretty much exactly the same as they had when they arrived. They climbed into the rear seats of the Jag with Shellby's man and their driver in the front.

"Right sunshine, show us what you got." Ronnie said, slapping the back of the passenger seat. The car pulled away into the yellow street lights and their tourist trip began. The city was smaller than the brothers had realised. Compared to London it seemed like one of the many small towns London had swallowed up in its centuries of expansion, but as Ronnie point out this was a good thing.

"Easy to control." He said imagining himself as a young Napoleon casting his eye across an already conquered city. The trip took them from the north side of Birmingham and the black areas of Handsworth, through to the other side of the city and the Irish quarter in Digbeth. All the time they talked about what they would change when they ran the place. After a couple of hours Reggie complained about his rumbling stomach and an Indian restaurant was chosen on the Old Bristol Road called *Days of the Raj* that, according to Shellby's man was the only Indian restaurant in town and would fill the gap. The brothers were intrigued having never sampled Indian cuisine before. Just as the four men were about to enter the restaurant Ronnie stopped at the doorway.

"You know what Reg, I ain't hungry. You carry on and stuff yourself Bruv. I'm gonna have a wander around. You know, get a feel for the place." Reggie knew what his brother had in mind and didn't press the subject any further.

"Alright Ron I'll wait here for you. Just be careful though this ain't London. They've probably never heard of us down here." With that the brothers parted. Reggie being lead by his hunger and Ron by his libido.

From Shellby's man Ron had worked out where the Trocadero was located and it turned out to be only a short walk from the restaurant. Ronnie wasn't used to homosexuals being so open about their sexuality. The London scene was much bigger but also much more in the spotlight due to the large amounts of celebrities and politicians that made up its number. The smaller more underground scene in Birmingham gave its participants much more freedom to carry on their lifestyle in a much more flamboyant way. No one really knew Ronnie Kray in Birmingham, and that suited him tonight. He walked into the dirty bar and struck up a conversation with the landlord. Ronnie explained he was only in town for one or two nights and needed a bit of help finding his way around. He asked about the city and its club scene and who the big names in town were. The landlord told him their wasn't a club scene to his knowledge. The only club in town was the Bermuda club and that was owned by the Fewtrells. Ronnie pressed the landlord for more information about the Fewtrells but the landlord didn't have anything else to tell him.

"I don't mind showing you around town darling." Ronnie turned to find a man with a red quiff standing next to him. Ronnie looked him up and down a smile growing across his face. "I know this town like the back of my hand dear. I'll even take you up the Bermuda club if you like. I know the Fewtrells I'll introduce you darling." Ron's eyes ran over the lean muscle on the man's shoulders and jaw. "Oh yea and what's your name then?" Ron asked.

"Me darling?" The man turned to face the Londoner. "They call me Jarvis. Everyone knows me and I know everyone." Ronnie held his hand out.

"I'm Ronnie mate. I can see I've bumped into the right person here." He half said to the landlord who was watching across the bar. " Let me get you two a drink." he said smiling. The two men sat next to each other two gin and tonics in hand. The conversation was riddled with sexual double entendres and flirtation. This carried on till neither man could stand it any more and Jarvis asked the landlord for the key to the back room. He held out his hand to Ronnie and led him into the darkened room where only a week or so before Micky Higgins had met his tormented death. Ronnie was a rough lover and that's how Jarvis liked things, but rarely had he met someone with such an aggressive and painful imagination. The sex didn't last long for either man. They had all night and both knew that this was only the first of such passionate moments. They emerged back into the front bar which was much busier now. Jarvis introduced Ronnie around and one or two thought they recognised him but he dismissed their approaches.

"I've gotta meet my brother Jarvis. Do you wanna tag along and give us the grand tour?" Jarvis was flattered.

"Yea that'd be great. If you keep the drinks coming I'll show you the town." Ronnie nodded in approval.

"You got a deal. Oh and I wanna see that Bermuda club too. As a matter of fact let's start there." Ronnie pulled a small tin from his pocket with twenty or so small blue pills inside. Ron picked one out and placed it in Jarvis's willing mouth. Jarvis looked around the bar at the other men watching and he sucked slowly on Ronnie's fingers. The other men gave a loud effeminate woo. Ron laughed embarrassed.

"You're a saucy facker Jarvis, I'll give you that mate." With that the two men finished their drinks and left smokey bar to make the rendezvous with Reggie.

Confrontation

Chapter 10

Eddie had the whole crew cleaning the club before opening time. Hazel and Don were organising the bar as Chrissy set the door up for the night. The younger brothers were making themselves useful wherever they could as well as chatting up the female bar staff. Fridays were always busy and although the club was small it always made plenty of cash over the weekend and if the next project was to go ahead they would need all the cash they could get. Hazel and Eddie had told the brothers about their idea for another club. They had to sell the idea of a big club with top names playing in Birmingham to the others. As they talked the brothers became more excited about the plan and Eddie had all but taken over the whole conversation by this point, making out that the whole thing was his idea. Hazel who was used to his exuberant manner let him carry on.

As the night began the brothers all worked with a new confidence. They felt that for the first time in their lives they had a chance at something legitimate.

Everything up until this point had been a blag. Not real. Even the Bermuda was illegal but the new club would drag them further away from the streets they had grown up in. Maybe even opening a door to the swinging sixties world they had read about in the papers and saw at the cinema.

The night started early. Couples showing up steadily over the first opening hour almost filling the club. Both Roulette tables were busy and much to Eddie's approval the cash had started to flow across the bar. His self appointed job in the club was to meet and greet. In other words smile, make them feel welcome and if necessary listen to any and all the bullshit that came out of their mouths, without losing that smile. But tonight he found himself covering most of the other jobs too. For some reason the brothers, Hazel and the rest of the staff just couldn't keep up with the amount of customers in the club. Between restocking the bar, collecting glasses, mingling with the customers and running back and forth answering and opening the front of club door the night had just run away with itself. Eddie glanced at the clock and it was nearly eleven o'clock. He decided to grab a whiskey from the bar and take a short break. Hazel who was helping out behind the bar poured the whiskey from the bottle freehand and dropped ice into the glass.

"There you go millionaire." she said sarcastically swilling the golden liquid around in the glass. Eddie took it smiling.

"Cheers bab." He glanced around the room. "If it carries on like this it won't be long till we *are* millionaires." Hazel smirked.

"Good, you can buy me that Merc you keep promising me Ed." He laughed, just as Eddie was about to answer her a tap on the shoulder brought his attention away from Hazel and back on the running of the club.

"Alright mate. Are you the owner?" Eddie turned to find a small group of well dressed men standing in front of him. Thinking that this was another sting by the police he answered

"No!" He pointed across the club to no one in particular. "He's over there mate." With that he downed the drink and slunk off into the packed room. Only looking over his shoulder after he was on the other side of the club. The group of men gathered around the bar and ordered drinks. Eddie saw Chrissy collecting glasses and grabbed his arm. "Hey Chrissy, do you think they're the old Bill?" Chrissy stood on his tip toes and looked around the bar until he found the group of men.

"Well if they are, then they're drinking on the job. So no they ain't the old Bill, but I do recognise one of em." He pointed to the slim man with the red quiff.

"Him, he's one of the Meat Market Mob. Queer too. So I'd say they're all queers." Eddie shook his head.

"*He* might be but the two in the black suits don't look like any queers I've ever seen." Chrissy laughed.

"Oh and you're an expert on this type of thing are you? All I know is that bloke with the red hair was there the night I had the trouble with Toddy Burns.The others weren't, but he was." Eddie frowned.

"Ok well just keep and eye on em."

Twenty minutes passed before the men approached him again.

"Ear mate, are you the boss here or not?" This time Eddie stopped what he was doing and turned full on to the group looking them over.

"Yea I'm the boss. Who wants to know?" Jarvis stepped forward.

"Are you Eddie Fewtrell?" Eddie frowned.

"Could be, but like I said who wants to know?" Jarvis gave a slimy smile and stepped to one side.

"I'd like to introduce you to Ronnie and Reggie Kray, two Brothers from London." Eddie held his hand out confused.

"Alright lads." Jarvis tried to continue but was pushed aside by Ronnie.

"Sorry about him mate. We've only just met him and he said he knew you." He said in a strong Cockney accent. Eddie looked Jarvis up and down and shook his head.

"No mate I've never laid eyes on him before. We don't normally get queers in here." He turned back towards the tall man in the black suit. "How can I help you gentlemen?" Ronnie and Reg came side by side in front of Eddie.

"No mate you've got it wrong. It's not how you can help us it's how *we* can help you." Both men gave a little, what seemed like rehearsed laugh.

"Oh yea," Eddie said intrigued. "and exactly how can you help me?" Reggie held his hand out.

"I'm Reggie." He said self-importantly. "Listen Eddie can we go somewhere a bit quieter so we can talk?" Eddie felt he was being pressured.

"No, here will do fine thanks. Talk about what?" The two Krays moved closer together blocking Eddie from the rest of the club.

"Protection Mr Fewtrell, that's what were talking about. We can look after you. Make sure no one moves in on your territory. Anyone causes you trouble we can sort them out for you." At first Eddie was stunned at the brothers' audacity. He stood frozen looking at the Krays open mouthed. The Londoners took it as a look of fear. But Eddie's silence was broken with a laugh.

"You two come down from London to protect me!" He said, in between laughing. The Krays looked at each other confused.

"Ronnie and I can protect you mate. We're brothers. Fighters!" Eddie continued to laugh. The Kray brothers began to get agitated. Jarvis spoke up poking his head between the men.

"It makes sense Eddie. You've got trouble coming and these gentlemen can help you out." Eddie's smiling face dropped instantly, suddenly totally serious.

"It's Mr Fewtrell to you, you queer cunt, and what do you mean I've got trouble coming?" Eddie slammed his fist into Jarvis's nose. The punch came fast and hard,his nose exploding. Jarvis fell backwards grasping his face. Blood pouring through his fingers, the Krays stepped back.

"Woah, hold on we didn't come here for trouble. We came to help you mate." Ronnie tried to reason but Eddie's face had changed to a manic grimace.

"You came to help *me?* You pair of Cockney ponces swan down from London thinking you're something and offer to protect fucking *me?*" Chrissy had been watching all along and with his warning the other Fewtrell brothers began to gather around the group of men blocking any chance of escape. Shellby's man tapped Reggie on the shoulder.

"We need to leave Mr Kray." Reggie agreed seeing the situation spiral out of control. Eddie continued his rant.

"Two brothers offer to protect *me*." Eddies thick Brummie accent getting higher pitched as he went on. "Let me tell you something you obviously don't fucking know. I've got *seven* brothers and we're *all* fucking fighters. So tell me what do I need you pair of cunts like you for?" Ronnie stepped forward.

"I'll take it that's a no then shall I?" He said trying to bluff his way through Eddie's aggression. Ronnie could feel that feeling of rage rising and was unfazed by the position he found himself in, he knew he had his brother to back him up and the pair of them made a formidable team. Reg placed his hand on Ronnie's shoulder and for the first time Ronnie saw the gathering group of Fewtrell brothers and their friends and realised the Londoners were outnumbered.

"You can take it how you fucking like pal." Eddie said pointing at Ron. Shellby's man tugged on Reggie's sleeve.

"Now, Mr Kray we've got to leave or this is going to go bad." Chrissy Fewtrell stepped forward.

"Who are you then? You ain't no cockney are ya?" He said pointing at Shellby's man. The man looked sheepishly at Chrissy.

"I work for Tom Shellby." He said expecting some recognition in the name. Chrissy shrugged his shoulders.

"Never heard of him mate, have you Ed?" He looked at Eddie.

"Yea, he used to have a gang here when our dad was a kid. Peaky Blinders, Race racket, but they're fuck all now." Ron and Reg looked shocked at hearing this. They had assumed Tom Shellby's gang still existed and held some sway in the city. Eddie came forward to Ronnie, face to face now.

"If you wanna have a pop at me, go ahead mate. I'll fight both of ya if you want, no one else will be involved" Eddie looked around at his brothers. "Did you here that? Just me and them." Ron nodded but Reg came in close to Ronnie's ear and whispered that there would be another time to deal with these northern wankers. "If that don't appeal to ya I'd suggest you both fuck off rather sharpish," he continued,

"and I don't just mean fuck off out of here. I mean fuck off out of Birmingham." Eddie dropped his voice to a whisper "If I find out you two are still in the city in two hours from now you're both gonna find out what it's like at the bottom of the grand canal. You won't be alone cos these other fuckers will be joining you."

The Krays backed away. Shellby's man leading the way through the crowd.

"This ain't over yet sunshine, not by a facking long shot." Ronnie backed away, his brother tugging his arm. Jarvis went to join them still holding his bleeding nose.

"Not you, you're staying here." Chrissy grabbed the man by his red hair and dragged him toward a seat, throwing him into it he turned and joined the rest of his brothers following the Londoners across the club until they disappeared through the front door of the building. Eddie opened up the small metal cage in the door and watched both the Krays climb into their Jag.

"Don, Frankie, follow them and make sure they know you're following them!" he said without turning to his brothers, still watching the grey car across the road. Don and Frankie Fewtrell did as they were told and headed out into the street. Don stood watching the Jag while Frankie walked down the hill to his car and climbed in. Revving the engine, Frankie pulled up behind the Jag and Don climbed in. The Jag pulled away quickly trying to lose the car behind it, but Frankie knew the roads and kept up easily. The Krays didn't bother returning to the Holiday Inn. They dropped Shelby's man off on the outskirts of Aston and headed straight for the M1 and London. Don and Frankie followed close behind until they reached the motorway.

"Ha I'd love to hear the conversation in that car on the way down south tonight." Don said laughing. Frankie looked across confused,

"What was it all about I missed it?" Don filled him in on the night's events.

"Them two ponces were offering *us* a protection racket and Eddie told them to go fuck emselves, basically." Don gave a shrug, "typical Eddie, always very diplomatic." Frankie laughed.

"But who were they Don? I mean they ain't just fell out the sky. They must be connected somewhere along the line. Maybe we're in for a bit of trouble from them at some point." Frankie turned the car back towards the city centre.

"Fancy a drink at the Elbow room?" Don looked at Frankie and they both burst out laughing again.

"Yea fuck it. We've done plenty tonight let's go down the Elbow room and see what the word is on them two cockneys. Someone must know em, there's always a few cockneys in there." The Ford Zephyr drove off in to the night across the city with both men in deep conversation about the night's events.

Back at the Bermuda business was back to normal. It wasn't the first time there had been a bit of argy bargy and to the Fewtrells who were used to such confrontations it was like water off a duck's back.

Chrissy had dragged Jarvis off to the office where he was told in no uncertain terms to sit and wait. No one knows what Eddie and Chrissy did to Jarvis that night. Any screams were drowned out by the music from the juke box down stairs. But whatever they did it was nothing in comparison to what Jarvis had poured out on poor Micky Higgins. In his torment we can only assume Duncan Jarvis admitted everything to Chrissy and Eddie. Because after the *interview* Chrissy told Eddie to call Dixie and tell him the man they had in their office had just admitted to killing Micky Higgins. He explained that he had seen the man in the back doorway of the Market Tavern as he and Micky had pulled away in Micky's van and how he had been the only person to have seen himself and Micky together on that night. Eddie slapped Jarvis around the face nearly knocking him off his chair.

"If you fucking move you're a dead man, understand? I mean it, one fucking move and you'll end up in the Earlswood Lakes, get it?" Jarvis floated in and out of consciousness and wasn't in any fit state to go anywhere. Chrissy went back down to the bar where he continued to help out at the Roulette tables. Eddie called Dixie and told him to get down to the club as fast as he could and explained the situation and told him not to come in his uniform as it might scare the customers. Dixie agreed. Jarvis sat chin on his chest, slowly coming around. The feeling of dread creating a hollow in his stomach bringing him back to his senses. Eddie went back on the door where people continued to arrive. Smiling he welcomed them in shaking hands and taking coats. Around two am Eddie peered through the gated hatch and saw a large group of men shuffling up the narrow ally. Eddie didn't see anything unusual about the group and swung the door open extending his hand to the first man smiling. Toddy Burns looked at the hand and ignored it walking straight past Eddie and into the club. The ten other men followed him.

"Alright lads." Eddie said smiling but none of the Meat Market Mob took any notice of him. Choosing to look at the floor as they walked past him instead. Eddie knew something was up but let them in anyway deciding to just keep an eye on them instead. He didn't have to wait too long to find out what the men had in mind. The group of men gathered around Toddy at the bar and ordered a large round of drinks with pints and shots to follow. Each man raised his glass and downed the shot then threw the glasses on the floor cheering. Hazel heard the smashing glass and marched to the end of the bar the men were standing.

"Oi!" She shouted over to the boozy men. "We'll have none of that shit in here boys." Toddy laughed.

"Fuck off slag." The other men burst into hysterics and without facing her continued, "Keep your mouth shut and get ten more shots like the last lot, sharpish or you'll get the back of my hand you mouthy bitch!" Although the other men were drunk Toddy knew what he was doing. As the words came out his mouth he scanned the room for anyone he recognised as a Fewtrell. Hazel, slightly dumbfounded as to what had just been said to her was, for once in her life lost for words. She convinced herself that she had misheard the tall man at the bar. She called over one of the bar staff and told them pour another ten shots for the group and told another to go around and sweep up the broken glass. Whilst the bar staff did this she went in search of one of the brothers for some back up. As she left the bar Hazel heard a cheer and turned to see one of the men trying to put his hand up the barmaid's skirt.

At this point it's best to explain that a bar fight in a movie is not the same as it is in real life. Especially when there are men involved that had been around violence all their lives. When you see an old black and white western movie with a hero in a white stetson punching someone who flies over a bannister rail and crashes to the floor only to jump up and continue fighting, that is just a fantasy. A real bar fight involves broken jaw bones, lost teeth embedded in fists, broken arms, legs and disfigurements that last a life time. Mental scars that fester in the brain like toxic dreams of revenge turning good men into bad. What happened that night in the Bermuda club has long since gone into Birmingham folklore.

By the time Hazel Fewtrell had returned to the bar the group of men had grown from ten to around twenty-five. Hazel had managed to get Chrissy who in turn had grabbed the other brothers. Eddie was still at the door shaking hands and smiling. Toddy had grabbed one of the barmaids and was molesting her for the entertainment of the other mob members; running his hand over her breasts whilst locked holding her paralysed in a neck hold. Chrissy burst into the group pulling Toddy's hand off the young crying girl. Toddy let her go. He smiled pleased with himself for finally managing to get some reaction from the Fewtrells. He wished Jarvis were here to witness what he and his boys were about to do. Toddy gave Chrissy a push.

"Oi," he laughed "get your own slag" The other men burst into laughter. Chrissy pushed back,

"You lot out now!" He said to no one in particular. Chrissy caught Toddy's eye and suddenly Chrissy knew who he was dealing with and this time there was no gun. For a second he was taken a back. The other brothers waited for his lead but he stood frozen. Without warning, one of the men stepped forward and slammed his fist into the side of Chrissy's jaw in a sucker punch that would've knocked a lesser man out. Chrissy fell forward but remained standing before another punch could be thrown Bomber, the youngest Fewtrell had thrown himself forward and landed his right fist into the man's nose breaking it and sending a fountain of blood splattering around the rest of the group. Chrissy, who had managed to pull himself back to his senses, had taken up a boxing stance alongside his two other brothers. The Meat Market Mob had gathered into a circle ready to fight. One of the customers ran out to warn Eddie that it was about to kick off in the bar and he ran into the bar and seeing the meat market boys had swelled in numbers he began searching for willing bodies to help in the fight to come. The two groups of men gathered facing each other. There was a small gap of about six feet in between them. Eddie came alongside his brothers and taking up the centre of the line he tried to reason with them,

"Alright lads," he almost pleaded, thinking of the damage to the club more than fearing the fight. "We don't want any trouble. Everyone's having a good night. Why ruin it with a rumble?" He looked around the faces of the men but didn't recognise anyone. "Let's shake hands and I'll get you all a drink." Toddy stepped forward.

"Fuck you and fuck your drink. You and your scumbag family are gonna get battered for what you did to Micky Higgins." Chrissy spoke up.

"We got Micky's killer *upstairs* in the office; one of your queer mates, Duncan Jarvis and he's told us everything. The Old Bill are on their way to arrest him now!" The news hit Toddy hard. The rest of the men looking around at each other shocked. Toddy knew he only had one way out of this situation now. If Jarvis had talked to the Fewtrells then he would also have no qualms talking to the police. Toddy picked up an empty beer jug and threw it at Eddie's head. Eddie saw it coming and ducked but the glass shattered into the face of the man behind him. He fell screaming, the first of many that night. Pandaemonium is the only word to describe the scene that followed. The men piled into each other, arms flaying around in round house punches; fists slamming into eyes, noses and teeth. Eddie had been hit over the head with a bar stool which knocked him to the floor before breaking into firewood around him. His assailant leapt down upon him grabbing him around the neck. Eddie pushed his hand into the man's throat squeezing his adam's apple as hard as he could, not knowing if he was doing any damage or not. His other arm searched the floor for a weapon. He found a broken part of the chair that moments before had smashed into his shoulders. Picking it up he saw the sharpened end of the broken piece of wood and slammed it onto the man's ear. The man squealed, releasing his grip on Eddie and falling to the floor trying, but unable to pull the wooden shard which was deeply embedded from his ear. The sight of the squealing man brought Eddie back to his surroundings. He sat on the floor and shook his head. All around him men were fighting. Chaos reigned. He saw Chrissy fighting his hardest against two or three men, holding his own whilst all around him glasses smashed and tables and stools were used as weapons by the other men. Screams of women and breaking glass filled the room and Eddie raised himself from the floor, stiff from the blow from the stool. He looked across to find Hazel in the melee, she had gathered the barmaids around her and was moving them towards the other end of the bar, sheltering them from the flying beer glasses. Eddie raised himself and within seconds had become part of the mass of violence. For every punch he threw he was hit three times and although his punches were powerfully landed, with men falling on the end of his fist he just couldn't seem to get on top of the situation. He saw Bomber his youngest brother under foot, desperately trying to regain his feet only to be punched and kicked back down to the blood soaked floor. In between blows Eddie took stock of the situation. He could see Chrissy cornered by several men holding his own but starting to tire out. Where were Frankie and Don? Their presence would swing the balance. Even with help of the customers who had joined in the battle, it slowly began to dawn on Eddie they were losing the fight and that would mean losing their foothold in Birmingham. The scenario of being poor again ran through his head. He could not allow that to happen. He fought harder, working his way over to Chrissy. Bomber was back on his feet now and although only twenty, he could fight like a man twice his size. Gordon and Johnny had helped him back to his feet and the three brothers fought back to back as they had done all their lives.

Eddie dragged himself to the corner Chrissy held, followed by the other brothers. They and whichever friends and customers were still standing fought hard, backs against the wall. Some of the Meat Mob had come armed with billy clubs smuggled into the club under their coats. A particularly nasty weapon made from a two foot rounded piece of wood, with nails driven into it protruding twenty centimetres either side. Almost medieval, it gave a devastating blow that drove the nails through the scalp, just piercing the skull allowing blood onto the brain. Not killing a man but maiming him in all sorts of ways. They put the clubs to good use as soon as the Fewtrells were cornered bringing the blows down around them. The brothers' friends fell fast and the Fewtrell line thinned out quickly. Eddie found himself face to face with one of the billy clubs, as the club came down he raised his arm for protection. The nails drove through silver mohair of his suit jacket into the muscle of his forearm, right to the bone. The pain was instant and intense, filling him to the core. He couldn't stand another blow like that. Eddie looked around for something to defend himself with but there was nothing. Leaping onto a table he kicked the man with the club, who fell back momentarily but then instantly sprang back to his feet like a cat to deliver the coup-de-grace. From his elevated position Eddie could see over the head's of the fighters. As he fought off the club-man another of Toddy's boys threw a pint jug at his head. Eddie saw it coming and caught it with both hands before it could smash into his face. The club-man came in for the kill. Eddie held the jug by the handle and brought the jug down hard on the man's head. Eddie's aim was off, mistiming his blow bringing the glass down too early, it caught the man in the face slicing his nose off completely and taking his top lip with it, as it shattered in to his face. The man fell back into the melee clutching the place where his nose had been, his screams turning to a burble as he began to choke on his own blood. Eddie was left holding the glass handle to the jug. He thew it to the floor grabbing a man by the hair he threw himself back into the fight, fists flying. In between punches and blows Eddie searched the room for Toddy Burns but couldn't see him anywhere.

Toddy had slipped away at the peak of the fighting when he could see the Fewtrells backed in to a corner and he assumed the fight was won. He ran behind the bar grabbing Hazel by her black hair and squeezed her face.

"Where's Jarvis Bitch?" Hazel froze. Toddy gave her a back hander across the face. "Where's the office? Take me there now!" Her bleeding lips shivered. He led her from behind the bar still keeping a tight grip on her hair forcing her up the stairs. "Move it slag." She opened the door to the office where Jarvis had been sitting, bleeding and waiting. Toddy threw Hazel across the office turning his attention to Jarvis. "What have you been saying you silly bastard?" Jarvis shook his head trying to talk, his lips caked in blood.

"I never told em anything Boss I swear." Toddy grabbed his red quiff.

"You told em enough. You told em about Higgins." Toddy's head swam with rage. The Fewtrells have told the Old Bill and now they know about you and that's too close to me for comfort." Hazel jumped to her feet and made a run for it but Toddy moved fast and blocked her exit. "Where you going darlin'?" grabbing her by the throat he forced her back across the office desk. "You don't wanna go back down there darlin; much too noisy." Toddy spun her around, forcing her to bend across the table. "Let's make ourselves a bit more comfortable shall we," he said grabbing her hair and wrapping it around his wrist. He tore her blouse around her shoulders. Hazel, wide eyed, realised his intentions and began to fight back, kicking backwards into Toddy's shins.

"EDDIE!" she screamed. Toddy's grip tightened. She felt his hand raising her skirt. Jarvis had begun to stir and Toddy told him to hold her down. Jarvis struggled to grab her wrists.

"Let me go you bastards. My husband's gonna kill you both." Hazel shouted more angry than scared. She heard toddy's trouser zip being undone. She braced herself for what was to come. But . . . nothing happened. The two men were talking. Hazel still held tight by Toddy's massive hand around her neck, began to come out of her panic, becoming aware of the other sounds going on around her. A gun shot rang out downstairs.

"There it is again!" Jarvis let go of Hazel's wrists and she wriggled out of Toddy's grip. She collapsed to the floor and crawled under the desk but she needn't had bothered. Both men had forgotten she was even there. Toddy grabbed Jarvis by his shirt collar. "Come on we're out of here!" The door slammed and she was on her own, tears welled up and she allowed herself to cry for minute. She crawled back out from under the desk and checking the two men had gone, she dried her eyes. She took a minute to do her hair in the office mirror and hiding any sign of weakness she stepped out into the corridor and walked back down the stairs shutting the fire exit door the two men had used to make their escape on her way.

The fight was over. The club was wrecked. The Fewtrells had won but at what cost? Dixie had shown up truncheon in hand flaying it around like some modern day knight. Then some of the Irish who had left Micky Higgins' wake for a late one arrived at the club only to find the front door open and, much to their delight a battle happening inside. They leapt into the fight, shouting gaelic battle cries, kicking and punching the hell out of anyone who got in their way. It was the return of Don and Frankie from the Elbow room though that swung the balance in their favour, not because they had made a difference with their muscle. Don didn't even throw a punch, he just pulled the old Lugar from his pocket and fired two shots into the ceiling and the deafening sound stopped the proceedings instantly.

The irony was lost on everyone. The gun that had started the fight had in the end brought it to a close. The Market Mob lay around, battered and blue. The ones that were still standing were ordered to kneel by Don, who had all but taken over the room by himself, pointing the pistol at all and sundry and talking tough. Not that the Fewtrells had come off any better. Eddie was gripping his arm which had been pierced like a pin cushion, blood seeping through his jacket sleeve turning the silver mohair deep claret. He was better off than most. Now the fight was over, and adrenalin levels had dropped, men who had their skulls, noses or arms broken and due to adrenalin or maybe because of the french blues or some other speed, had carried on scrapping regardless, were now starting to feel the pain that had been inflicted by the brutal fighting. Slowly moans started to fill the room. Dixie asked Eddie if he wanted the police involved. Eddie said that he didn't but assured him that any one of the Meat Market Mob who stepped through his doors again was a dead man and he also made this fact clear to the kneeling men, before they were punched and kicked, bleeding and moaning out onto the cold street.

Hazel found Eddie, they hugged a while before she started to attend to his wounds. Chrissy sat with them on one of the few chairs that still had legs. Everyone was quiet, talking in muted tones, attending to each other. The Irish lads asked if they could have a drink and Eddie obliged asking the barmaids to get everyone drinks on the house.

"Where's the bloke you called me about?" Eddie pointed towards the stairs not looking up.

"He's in the office Dixie, Duncan Jarvis, he admitted everything. Bang the fucker up!" Dixie began towards the stairs but Hazel interrupted.

"He's gone Dix. That big bloke came and got him. They went out the Fire escape, cowardly bastards." She turned her attention to the bar staff, taking her mind off what had nearly happened upstairs and made sure everyone had drinks. Dixie and Eddie went upstairs anyway whilst the others began picking up the broken furniture and glass. Both roulette tables were ruined, smashed beyond repair. Chrissy, Don, Bomber, Gordon and Frankie looked over the ruins of what was the Bermuda club, before following the other two upstairs.

"So what happened?" Dixie asked. Eddie told him about the Londoners who had accompanied Jarvis into the club earlier that night trying to get a protection racket started.

"That little Scouse queer knew this was coming." Eddie sat in his office chair spitting blood from a missing tooth into the bin. "You think he had something to do with all this?" Dixie continued. Chrissy took up the conversation.

"This was just the Market boys trying to muscle in is all." Eddie stood up

"Don't be soft Chrissy. This was those Cockney bastards." His paranoia taking hold. "Don't you think it's a bit of a coincidence that we get muscled in on from them two London wankers, and two hours later the club gets wrecked? . . . For fuck's sake wake up. This was them Kray twins." Eddie had Dixie's attention now.

"Kray twins you say. . . . *The* Kray twins from London were here?" Dixie had gone white. All the brothers turned toward Dixie. "*The* Kray twins. What do you mean *The* Kray twins." Don spoke up for the first time. Eddie turned on him.

"Where the fuck were you two anyway?" He cuffed Don's ear. "If you two had been here there wouldn't have been a problem would there?" Eddie fronted Frankie and Don up but Dixie stepped in between them.

"Stick to the subject at hand Eddie. If you had the Krays in from London tonight then you've got big problems!" He looked around the room. Everyone was non plussed. "Don't you read the fucking papers?" Still no reaction from the brothers except blank looks and shrugs.

"Frankie cant read at all." Chrissy joked trying to break the somber mood.

"Fuck you." Frankie laughed in his deep Brummie brogue. Dixie wasn't laughing.

"Jesus lads, the Krays run most of London. Don't you know this? They've got the biggest protection racket in the country and they ain't got one club like you have they've got their grubby mits on twenty or thirty fucking clubs." He let the words sink in. "Obviously they're trying to move into Birmingham and someone's put you name at the top of the list." Don spoke again.

"Let em fucking try. We saw em off this time we can do it again." Dixie sat on the desk and took a long drink from the whisky he'd been handed.

"No Don, you're not getting this," he explained slowly, "these fuckers are proper killers. They'll send assassins from London to come and shoot you." The brothers were silent. "They'll turn the other gangs and families of Birmingham against you. You're all gonna have to watch your backs. If they were behind this tonight then you know they ain't fucking around." Eddie stood up.

"Tom Shellby. He's the one who's fingered us. He's making moves to take control of the city again through the Kray twins. If what Dixie says is true then we seem to have a fight on our hands." Chrissy put his hand on Don's shoulder and looked at Eddie.

"Thank god Don had his gun." Don pulled the revolver from his pocket smiling. Dixie shook his head.

"I didn't see that ok? I'll lose me job if that's found. You need to get rid of it." Don nodded even though he had no intention of doing any such thing.

"Yea Don, where did you get that anyway, it's a fucking antique?" Eddie put his hand out for the gun. Don slapped the gun into Eddie's hand.

"Well this antique saved your arse tonight didn't it?" trying to hide his hurt feelings. Chrissy patted Don's shoulder.

"Yea Dons right we'd have been fucked if he hadn't had it." Eddie took the gun and placed it into the old black safe that sat under his desk. Dixie turned to Eddie.

"I'll speak to my Superintendent, tell him what's going on. I've got a bit of sway down the station now. Oh, and by the way you didn't need to ask me to come in *plain* clothes cos that's what I wear all the time now. Thanks to your tip offs they've made me a detective" Eddie looked embarrassed. He knew the other brothers wouldn't approve of his tip offs.

"If you can't beat em you gotta use em." Eddie said trying to save face. He raised his glass.

The other brothers and Dixie joined him. The men stood in the small office, arms raised, bleeding from the fight bringing their glasses together in the middle of the circle they had formed. Eddie said the blood oath.

"Whatever happened tonight, whatever or whoever comes at us. We ain't going nowhere. We'll rebuild this club and open the new one, and after that we'll open another and another until we run this fucking city. If the Krays, Peaky Blinders, Meat Mob or any other bastards think they can come into this city and take us on just let them fucking try. Things are gonna change. We are never gonna get in this situation again. We've got to build; bring things together, stop fucking around. This ain't a game no more. These fuckers are out to kill us so we gotta stay sharp. If we let just one of those bastards get a foot hold here, we're fucked. There's gonna be blood and plenty of it, but we gotta show strength, send a message out to all the other gangs out there that think they can move in on our pitch. *Birmingham belongs to us.*"

Fish bait

Chapter 11

If you travel out of Birmingham town centre on the Old Pershore Road, you'll go through two villages. These days the villages are part of the spiralling mass that is Birmingham, joined together to form one area due to the huge housing estates that plugged the gaps between them that have been built since the seventies. Early in the sixties they were two distinct separate villages; Stirchley and Cotteridge. In between the two villages is a little road called Lifford Lane. At that time you would be forgiven for thinking you were travelling down a country lane due to the over-hanging trees and grass verges. Halfway down the road is a beautiful Tudor manor house called Lifford Hall and directly behind the hall is Lifford reservoir, a rectangular, man made lake surrounded by huge oak trees. When sat beside the lake you might think you were in the middle of the countryside, but this is just subterfuge because right behind the trees hides the city. In fact, on one side of the reservoir is one of the biggest housing estates in Birmingham and on the other side is one of the city's largest rubbish dumps.

All types of rubbish can be found there: old prams, fridges, rusted out wrecks of cars, but the week after the fight at the Bermuda club a silver GS Vespa was dumped there. To the young school boys that climbed over the fence in the night to steal odds and sods from the tip there was nothing wrong with it. They couldn't for the life of them work out why anyone would dump a perfectly good motor scooter and couldn't believe their good luck at finding such a trophy. Hauling it over the fence they made off with it, three up on the little seat. A knife was jammed and turned inside the ignition and a small kick on the kickstart brought the little 150cc engine to life. The rest of the night was spent riding the little Vespa up and down the canal side walkway at break neck speed. The little engine blowing out clouds of sweet smelling, purple two-stroke smoke. This went on for hours until the young men had become tired of their new toy and wanting to finish what had been an eventful evening for them, they drove the little GS vespa at full speed into the canal, making a huge splash and a rousing a happy cheer from the young hoodlums.

On the same week the young ne'er do wells had their fun with the scooter, the fishermen that sat around the reservoir casting reeling and casting again, they had caught nothing for weeks. The carp and pike that the lake was famous for with local fishermen had found other food. Of course nobody could have known this at the time, but the big fish were happy eating whatever they could from the bottom of the lake and this week, there was plenty. Years later when the lake was drained for repairs a skeleton was found, partially eaten and partially preserved by the weeds, a plastic shopping bag tied around the head. The skull had a crack in it, as if a meat clever had been broken the bone and crushed the brain inside. The victim of this vicious assault was never identified. Whomever had killed the poor bag of bones had taken the trouble to remove all the teeth from the jaw bone, making it harder to identify, if ever it were found. The police who handled the removal and investigation of the bones were intrigued to find the skull had been wrapped in a plastic bag and this had helped to preserve some of the skin that made up the top of the scalp. On that thin layer of skin coating the skull was a shock of red hair.

A good day for the Gypsies

Chapter 12

Work had begun on the warehouse. It was slow at first. Walls had to be taken down and metal girders had to be inched into place to hold up the building. But after weeks of dirty work the brothers finally had something that resembled a night club. What the Fewtrells lacked in skill they more than made up in enthusiasm. The name for the club still evaded them and Eddie's idea to name it after himself was met with piss-taking. This made him decide not to mention it again although he still thought *Edwards No1* was a great name for his new venture. Hazel had decided to take over the interior design, but this would prove to be expensive and she didn't relish telling Eddie her ideas as they would undoubtedly be refused by the evermore penny pinching *Edward* Fewtrell, as he had now started calling himself.

During the build the word had gone out around town about the visit from the Kray twins and how the Fewtrells, especially Eddie had seen them off. The story began to take on a life of its own. Exaggeration making the confrontation out to be something more like a gladiatorial event between the Londoners and the local under dogs. The fight with the Meat Market Mob after the meeting with the Krays hardly got a mention. Eddie was hailed a Brummie hero; a lone working class lad, standing up against the overwhelming odds to these London gangsters trying to take over the city. The story was made all the more interesting to locals because of the immense national media coverage of the Krays mixing with celebrities at their clubs in the capital, which had turned them into celebrities themselves. Of course, Eddie and the rest of the brothers knew that the trouble with the Krays had just begun and there were other, more local, equally vicious gangs that would have to be battled before they could relax. Any rumours that increased their reputation as a family not to be messed about with were to be encouraged. However behind the strong words and bravado there was an unspoken fear which made the Fewtrell brothers work a little bit harder, dig a little bit deeper and push a little further to get the club finished.

They had also put the Bermuda club back together. The damage caused by the fight looked far worse than it actually was. The physical and mental damage to those that took part in the battle would take much longer to clear up. Punters were still coming in and spending and if anything, the place had got busier due to the word of mouth publicity, but there was a feeling amongst the brothers that it was time to move on; get out before it all came tumbling down. There was an underlying worry that the dodgy foundations the club was built on were slowly crumbling away and if they didn't move quickly the financial ground under their feet would just disappear. Dixie had been warning them that there were mutterings and a desire around the station to shut the club down. The police thinking was that The Krays would stay out of Birmingham if the Fewtrells would just go away. In the next few months their thinking would turn take a U-turn.

Billy Smith was from one of the large gypsy families that camped around the outskirts of Birmingham. The gypsy community at that time still had its feet firmly in the traditional way of life unchanged for hundreds of years. Many of them still lived the old way, in horse drawn, barrow top vardo wagons, eating around camp fires along little lanes and stopping places that had been used by the gypsies for centuries. The younger gypsies had begun to move into the new styled trailers, huge doubled wheeled caravans covered in chrome and ornate cut glass. Billy Smith was one of these new breed. Happy to mingle or trade with the house dwellers or as they called them *Gorgies,* always on the move and always on the make. Billy had become friends with the Eddie Fewtrell after meeting him at the Birmingham Rag market. The pair had come up with scams together over many frothy coffees at their stalls and a good friendship was built around who could come up with the best way to relieve people of their cash.

Billy Smith had moved on to better things since the Rag Market days and had just bought himself a sixty by eighty foot marquee. He intended to make a move into the circus business. He had put the word out among the gypsy community that he needed wood for the benches and plenty of it, so for weeks after building sites and wood yards were pilfered for anything that resembled a plank of wood. After two weeks he had more wood than he could ever use and more was still coming in from his ever resourceful gypsy friends so Billy decided to sell on what was left and start buying his props and acts.

The early sixties was a time when if you had the cash then you could pretty much get anything you wanted on the still vibrant, black market left over from World War Two. Billy Smith wanted wild animals and lots of them. One of the first animals he bought was a small black bear called Barnaby. The Romanian show-people who sold him Barnaby were about to head back to their own country and were only to happy to be rid of the bear. As the animal grew he was eating more than they could earn or steal and, being very superstitious people, they had come to look upon the bear as being jinxed. They blamed it for a run of recent bad luck and financial strife, or at least that's what they told Billy. Firstly their main reasons for moving the bear on was their inability to stop the bear shitting anywhere and everywhere it wanted to, and with the amount of food he was eating, there was a lot of shitting going on. The second and main reason was the bear had reached the age when he was no longer a pup and would in the next six months grow into a six foot tall 600 pound black bear, not something you would want in a small horse drawn caravan.

Billy bought the bear and after a short while the animal and Billy had grown very close, with Billy making it wear one of his waistcoats, amongst other clothing items. His intention was to have the little bear as a meet and greet attraction at the big top. His suspicions that the bear might not be the right choice as the first attraction the public saw when entering the Circus tent were compounded every time the bear took to crapping in the middle of his pristine Vickers caravan, sending his wife into fits, and stinking out the trailer for hours. Gypsy women are not known to be outspoken when it comes to their husbands' decisions but Billy's other half told him, in no uncertain terms, that she would move in with her mother if the bear didn't go. The shame of such a thing happening was too much for Billy Smith's gypsy honour. After Billy heard of the Fewtrells' new club under construction, he decided to pay Eddie a visit with four tonne of cedar wood planks that were too good to use on his new circus seating. Billy drove the old Bedford flat-bed himself with the planks neatly piled on the back and Barnaby sitting shotgun in the dirty cab.

Eddie and the other brothers looked over the wood and decided to go for it and the haggling started in earnest. After nearly two hours the price couldn't be settled and it looked like it was going to come to blows. The Fewtrells wouldn't let him leave with the wood and Billy wouldn't sell the wood at the price they were offering and so a stand off had been reached. This is where Barnaby the bear entered the negotiations. The bear who had been sitting patiently in the driver's cab wearing his blue trilby and red neckerchief and one of Billy's old waistcoats. Billy had trained the animal to wear them and now the poor bear was inseparable from said fashion items. The bear in the cab became bored of listening to the raised voices and decided to join in, forcing the half open window down completely he climbed out of the cab, strolled over to Billy took his hand and sat beside him looking like some weird little hairy man in his Sunday best.

Jaws dropped. Silence came over the negotiations.

"What the fuck is that?" Bomber stood pointing at the little hair ball in a hat.

"Is it a Pygmy?" he said astonished. Billy burst into laughter. "It's a bloody bear you ingrate." Billy stepped back from Barnaby and started to clap his hands. The bear on hearing the rhythm started to dance in small circles on his hind legs. Eddie joined Billy clapping, a huge smile growing on his face. The other brothers joined in now and the bear spun round like a whirling dervish, cute little grunts coming from his toothless mouth. The laughter and clapping grew and grew.

Tears rolled over cheeks and the Fewtrell brothers became hysterical. Eddie sat down exhausted his cheeks hurting.

"Stop him. Stop him for fucks sake my sides are killing me!" Billy grabbed the bear's collar and brought him to his side.

"Sit down Barnaby!" he commanded, much to Billy's relief the bear obeyed. The mention of the bear's name brought another round of laughter.

"Fucking Barnaby." Bomber said, pointing at thee animal laughing.

"He's called fucking *Barnaby*!" The bear sat down as if nothing had happened. Billy dug into his pocket and pulled out a rustling package of greaseproof paper. Unraveling the paper he pulled out a half eaten sandwich and gave it to the bear. Barnaby took the sandwich and crushed it between his hands turning it to mush before popping the whole thing in his mouth and chewing it in his toothless jaws. Eddie knew a good thing when he saw it.

"I'll pay you the price you want for the wood as long as the bear is thrown in." Billy gave a sad smile towards the bear and increased his price by one hundred pounds. "SOLD!" shouted Eddie.

Billy Smith drove the old Bedford flat bed back to the stopping site alone. Only allowing himself a smile when he was well out of sight of the Fewtrells. His plan had worked. The wood had been hard enough to trade but he knew as soon as Eddie and his brothers saw the dancing bear the negotiations wouldn't last too long. He had made himself a good deal of money, got rid of the shitting bear, kept his wife and his honour amongst the travelling folk.

A good day for the gypsies.

A job offer

Chapter 13

Toddy Burns had gone to ground after the fight. The Meat Market Mob was over, he knew that. The best fighters were either under arrest and awaiting sentencing or too injured to be of any use anymore. The disappearance of Toddy during the fight hadn't gone unnoticed either. The lads blamed the lack of Toddy for their losing the fight in the end. There was even talk of getting even with their former leader, but most of the mob were being watched by the police so couldn't make a move and even if they could Toddy was nowhere to be found. Toddy had heard all the talk, at first defending himself against the gossip but in the end the more he said the worse the murmurings around the market had become. He sat in his house ignoring the doorbell, stewing over the events and how things had played out. Jarvis was gone. That hurt more than he thought it would, but at least he hadn't been pulled in by the Old Bill about Micky Higgins.

"That queer had a big mouth," he told himself justifying the situation he found himself in, sooner or later he would've talked to someone or other and that would've brought the whole house of cards down on his head, he *had* to do something to stop Jarvis yapping. Drinking seemed to be the only release for him now. His wife and children had left him. She had showed her concern for his depression and night horrors and when he couldn't find the words to explain himself, he turned to using his fists on her instead, beating her black and blue in front of the children. For the kids though the separation from their father was a blessing in disguise. No more visits by *Uncle* Duncan. No more beatings or back handers.

He heard about the Krays' visit. Everyone was talking about it and so, after two weeks he found himself sitting on the train to London in his Sunday best. He didn't know who or how to contact the twins, but he knew that the Krays and he had one thing in common; their mutual hatred of the Fewtrells. He was going to offer to settle the score.

Apart from his spell in the army on National Service, where he'd served his tour in Algeria and even seen a bit of action, Toddy had never been outside of Birmingham in his life, and since his return from the army had never found any reason to go outside the city limits, until now. When the big blue and yellow diesel pulled up at Victoria station he was a little bit dumb struck. The amount of people buzzing around was enough to make you dizzy. Birmingham was a thriving city but London was something else entirely. He wandered out into the street and was greeted by the deafeningly glorious sound of a million people going about their business: buses, cars, scooters, whizzing here and there. Suddenly Toddy felt very old fashioned. His old suit was out of fashion in *Birmingham* but here he looked like something from out of an old war film. He hailed a taxi and headed to Carnaby Street, the only place in London he had ever heard of, thanks to the expose in the Sunday papers about the new youth cult calling themselves *Mods*. If he was going to meet the Krays and they were going to take him seriously he needed to look the part. The taxi dropped Toddy at the end of Carnaby Street. The contrast of style and colour compared to Birmingham's grey shades made Toddy realise just how small Birmingham really was. If he could get in with Krays he would move down here. He allowed himself to dream a little.

The shops were full of all sorts of clothes in colours that you wouldn't be seen dead in, *in Birmingham.* The Mods were everywhere, arriving and leaving on Vespas and Lambrettas adorned with a multitude of chrome lights, mirrors and badges, the names of their gangs of London areas written in golden lettering on the fly screens above the little headlights. Every now and then a sports car would pick its way down the street, stopping the pedestrians who were gathered in small groups along the road, in smart bright suits and green army parka,s smoking and drinking coke, eyes wide with amphetamine excitement. The place felt alive. There was a buzz in the air that you could almost touch. Toddy felt very old all of a sudden, even though he had only just turned thirty. After an hour of window shopping he finally settled for a silver mohair, three button, small lapelled suit in the new mod style, similar to the one Eddie Fewtrell had been wearing on the night of the fight. One hair cut and a shave later and he looked the part. He was ready to introduce himself to the Krays.

The Krays weren't too hard to find. Ask any London cabbie in the 1960s and they all had a story to tell about who had done this or that and how they looked after their own. Toddy found himself in a street of houses in the fashionable area of Knightsbridge. The taxi pulled up outside a normal looking house.

"Ear ya go mate," the Cabbie leaned over the seats. "Esmerelda's Club."

Toddy looked for a sign but there was none. The taxi driver pointed down to the cellar of the building. "Down there mate!" leaning further over the seats he tapped the meter. Toddy handed over the money and stepped out onto the road. The place was silent. The cabbie wound his window down,

"You're a bit early mate, this place won't get going until midnight." Toddy turned and smiled.

"Any pubs around here then?" "Yea jump in I'll take ya," a smile growing on the cabbie's face. "Fuck that!" Toddy laughed. "Your last little tourist excursion cost me enough I'll walk mate."

"Find the fackin pub yourself then!" The Cabbie's smile dropped and he drove off winding his window back up, muttering obscenities. Toddy stood for a second taking in the silence of the street. Beyond he could hear the grind and hum of London, but here it was tranquil and that helped to calm his nerves. He put his hands in the pockets of his new suit and began walking down the road to find his bearings. He felt like he'd been born again. Like he was part of something bigger than the Meat Market Mob and all that Brummie stuff. This was the real deal. If he could convince the Krays that he could deal with the Fewtrells then they might offer him a place in the Firm.

Ten minutes later he was sat in the Wilton Arms resting against the bar, beer in hand and a whiskey chaser waiting in front of him. He had butterflies, the first time since he was a boy playing his first football match for his local team. The beer helped, yes he was a little bit scared but he tried to look upon it as a business meeting. The more he drank, the more he convinced himself of the outcome of his to meet the Krays. He was sure they would welcome him with open arms.

Slowly the pub filled with people in their late twenty, early thirties. Toddy continued to drink watching the flamboyance around him. After a while he realised they were all going to Esmereldas club at closing time. He began to relax and he even struck up a few conversations with the punters, small talk mainly but he was quite open about meeting the Krays. The people he talked to assumed he was part of the Firm and treated him with respect and he let them believe whatever they wanted.

Esmerelda's Club was a plush but small club. The place was a very fashionable club to be seen in amongst the multitude of celebrities that enjoyed getting a bit of street credibility by hanging out with, what they considered a *rougher* sort. Although, when he arrived the Krays were elsewhere in the city. After a short chat with the manager about who he was and why he was there, phone calls were made and after a short wait two well dressed men turned up and took Toddy to a small booth. A bottle of champagne was put in front of him by a beautiful young blonde girl who asked him to open the bottle and then joined him, drinking and flirting. All the time the two men stood outside of the red velvet curtains separating the booth from the rest of the club.

Toddy was totally oblivious to this, concentrating instead on the beauty in front of him. The young girl became more seductive and Toddy let her do whatever she wanted, using her hands and mouth to his delight. London was washing over him, seducing him, pulling him in. Now he'd had a taste he wanted more. He would do whatever he had to if it meant that he could become part of this. For the first time he understood the term *swinging sixties* he'd heard so many times in the news.

The Kray twins arrived an hour later. The brothers walked into the booth and sat either side of Toddy. The girl got up and left, Reggie patted her arse as she passed taking the champagne with her. The two men filled the red velvet booth. The curtains contrasting against their matching black suits. They sat leaning forward hands on their knees. Toddy pulled himself together, tucking his shirt back into his trousers and straightening his tie, trying to sober up. Ronnie talked first.

"We've been told your from Birmingham and you know the Fewtrells. Is that right?" His tone was not friendly.

"Yea that bastard Eddie Fewtrell killed my best mate." Toddy lied.

"Killed your best mate you say. So what's that got to do with us?" Reggie sat drumming his fingers on his knee.

"My best mate Duncan Jarvis. They killed him. They killed Micky Higgins too. Those fuckers have to pay for what they did." Toddy continued the lie and decided to demonise the Fewtrells as much as he could. Ronnie took over.

"And this is of interest to us because?" He left the question hanging, Toddy decided to make his move.

"You . . . The Krays want to get into Birmingham but the Fewtrells are stopping you. Well, I can help you." Now Toddy sat back and took a drink hoping the twins wouldn't see his hand shaking.

"Ok now you've got our attention. What's your name son?" Ronnie held his hand out.

Toddy extended his hand and introduced himself. He took Ronnie's surprisingly soft hand and shook it hard. Reg just nodded and said,

"Firstly let's just get things straight. If we wanted Birmingham we'd just take it. The Fewtrells' ain't fack all. We could load up a few busses drive up there and just crush em. We don't need anyone's help."

"But!" Ronnie interrupted." The simplest way to do any job is from the inside which is were you come in." Ronnie stopped talking for a second."Duncan Jarvis was your best pal you say? Red quiff, queer?" Toddy was taken back.

"Red quiff, homosexual. Yea that's right. How do you know him?"

"He's the bloke that took us to the Fewtrells' club. He said he knew Eddie Fewtrell but it turned out to be bollocks. He didn't know fack all."

Toddy was speechless, thinking fast, he made a joke of how Jarvis was always saying he knew people he didn't, always trying to be popular. Ronnie's mind dwelled on the sex he'd enjoyed with the man in the back room of the Toreador hotel. He could see Jarvis was a ponce but felt he had a connection to the man so decided he would give Toddy the benefit of doubt. "You say he's dead. How did he die?"

"I don't know he just disappeared the night you visited the Bermuda club. No-one's seen him since." Reggie remembered the night.

"Yea they made him stay behind after we left." He turned his attention back on the Brummie in front of him.

"Ok Mr Burns why are you telling us this? How can you helps us?" Toddy just blurted it out.

"I'll kill Eddie Fewtrell for you. He's the main man. Once he's dead the others will just fold, especially if you move in straight after with some strong arm tactics. I know people in Birmingham, hard-men, willing to fight your corner . . . I'll kill him!"

There was a short silence between the men. For the first time Toddy noticed the thick chunky sound of a hammond organ playing in the background. The twins were talking amongst themselves now, but Toddy felt elsewhere. Maybe it was the champagne or just the moment was too intense, whatever it was he came back to reality when Ronnie tapped his knee.

"Have you ever killed anyone before Toddy?" The memories of Jarvis ran through his head.

"Yes twice, once in the army in Algeria the other with my bare hands. I ain't got a problem with it. Obviously I'll need a gun so you'll have to sort that and if I do this for you, you'll need to do something for me."

"Oh yea and what's that then?" Reg gave Ron a sideways look.

"If I kill Eddie Fewtrell I'll have to leave Birmingham forever. I'll need a job. Maybe you could find a position in your firm for me?" Toddy left the question hanging in the air, he pictured the words circling with the sound waves of the Hammond organ. Both the Krays started to laugh.

"Facking hell. I thought you were gonna ask for some money." Toddy kicked himself for not thinking to.

"Nah, just a job Mr Kray." Reg turned to Ronnie.

"I think we can find a position for a smart young man like you. What do you say Ron?" Ron turned to the curtains.

"Hey!" he called to no one in particular. "Get another bottle of champagne we're gonna celebrate a new member of the Firm." Turning to Toddy he gave a broad smile. "We'll get you a gun, something smooth, reliable and if you can *Kill* that Bastard Fewtrell you'll have a job waiting here when you get back. Welcome to the Firm Toddy." He held his hand out once more and grinned.

Toddy took his hand and smiled back but something inside him didn't feel right and although he was excited he couldn't help but wonder if he'd made a deal with the devil.

Toddy had the feeling that the brothers needed to talk amongst themselves so he excused himself to visit the toilet. Ronnie and Reg sat looking at each other. There was no need to talk they both knew instinctively what the other was thinking. Smiles grew on their faces as the scenario of Toddy Burns murdering Eddie Fewtrell ran through their minds.

"It's a win win situation." Ronnie broke the silence. "If that silly cunt what's to kill Eddie Fewtrell for us on the promise of a job then who are we to argue."

Reggie poured another drink from the champagne bottle.

"I'll get him a gun and well fack him off on the first train tomorrow back to Birmingham. If he shows up here and the jobs been done we'll put him on the door somewhere at one of the clubs."

Ronnie nodded. "Yea and if he doesn't, we'll throw the facker in the Thames."

Both brothers burst out laughing. Ronnie had that strange feeling again, he recognised it as excitement but in fact it was a deep psychopathic streak of cruelty. His mind began to work out ways to trick the Brummie.

"I know Reg let's give him a bit of what we got off the Yanks." Reg shook his head.

"Facking hell Ron you're like a kid in a sweet shop with that stuff." He nodded as if he were giving Ronnie permission, but in fact he was as curious as his twin to see how it affected Toddy. "Go on then!" Heroin was a virtually new leisure drug in Great Britain in the early 1960s. Although it had been around since the Victorian times it was mainly used medicinally in medicines such as laudanum as a cure for headaches, depression and a myriad of other physical and mental illnesses. Opium had been the main drug of choice in the Victorian period with the country even going to war with China over its supply, annexing Hong Kong in the process. Heroin was the dream drug dealer's product. Something new for the masses, one hundred times more addictive than nicotine. The jazz men down at Ronnie Scotts, Le Club Foot and the other Jazz clubs scattered around the West End were all into it and it had a cult following amongst the snaked eyed addicts. However, heroin had yet to escape on to the streets of England, and that was something Ronnie and Reg intended to correct. So for the Krays this was a case of product testing. The Americans had told them it was highly addictive and they had also tried it on some of the girls in the clubs who craved after it after only a few hits, turning them into slaves that would just about do anything for more of the off white powder. Now it was time to check it out on Toddy Burns.

Ronnie rose and talked to one of the men outside the booth, a phone call was made and then he peeked back into the small circular booth. Toddy had returned from the toilet and was already chatting with Reg. Ron called one of the working girls that frequented the club over to him, and instructed her to take care of their guest. She grabbed another bottle of champagne and strutted in to the booth plonking herself next to Toddy. Ron followed her and the four sat chatting like old friends.

After half an hour a skinny man in a scruffy long beige raincoat and french beret arrived. Ron and Reg made a big deal of the elderly man who smiled but didn't say a word to either of them. Toddy rose, shaking the man's hand. The man an American gave Toddy a big smile and looked friendly enough. Toddy noticed the man's teeth were almost black. Decay had eaten through them leaving tiny stubs sticking from the bright red gums and he had a sheen of cold sweat on his brow. Even though the man looked like tramp Toddy was impressed; the first American he'd ever met. Reg could see Toddy looking the man over and pointed out the man was a Jazz drummer, one of the best in the world. Toddy had never heard of him but pretended he had. The man sat next to Toddy and proceeded to delve inside his raincoat breast pocket. He pulled out a silver flat case about ten inches long and laying it on the table he opened it and lay it's contents out in front of him in a very particular order. Toddy was intrigued, as were the others. The American picked up a small pill box from inside the larger silver case and unscrewed the lid. The pill box was full of white powder with tiny brown specks. He took a tiny spoon and scooped out a small amount of the powder and lay it on a circular tray about four inches in diameter. He next took a small candle from the case, stood it on the table and lit it. Holding the silver tray up he poured a drop of champagne into the white powder and stirred it with the silver spoon until the liquid mixed with powder turning the liquid into a dirty brown colour. He passed Toddy and the girl two silver tubes. Toddy looked confused. The American gestured on how to hold it, placing the tube into his mouth like a cigarette and sucking air through it. Toddy and the girl put the tube up to their lips as instructed. The man then held the tray over the candle. The brown liquid began to sizzle and bubble turning it into a thick dark brown sludge. As it cooked it gave off an acrid smelling smoke. The man then took the tray away from the candle and held it up to Toddy and the girl's face. Once more gesturing for them to suck in the smoke, without questioning and caught up in the bravado of the moment, both of them leant forward. Toddy sucked. The dark smoke drew in through the little silver pipe through Toddy's mouth down his throat filling his lungs. Toddy only had time to put the pipe back onto the table before being washed away in a tidal wave of pleasure as the heroin chased into every corner of his body mind, releasing him from everything he had ever known: the club, The Krays, Eddie Fewtrell, Birmingham, his children, wife, Jarvis's murder, all of it was gone, replaced by a feeling of heavenly celestial pleasure.

He slumped back on the red velvet couch with a sleepy smile. His eyes were closed but he heard the Krays laughing and talking. Their voices seemed a long way away. His perspective had changed in a way he couldn't understand. Toddy knew his eyes were closed, but he was watching the whole scene from above now. He laughed to himself at the absurdity of it all. The grinding Hammond organ driving along modern jazz filled him now, only broken by the girl next to him giving a small gasps of sexual pleasure. Was he pleasuring her? He couldn't tell. Was that him lying on the couch? He tried to shake himself out of the stupor but instead felt as if he were sinking deeper into the red velvet, drowning in a continual orgasm and at that moment he gave himself to the beautiful feeling that ran through his veins. Happy to drown even if it meant death. For the first time in his life he knew now this was how his life should always be. This was his path.

When he awoke, the music, the Krays, the girl and the American had all gone. He was alone in the club in the dark. He sat there for a while savouring the peaceful feeling he felt within. The heroin still soaked through him but the sleepy feeling had gone. He now just felt fulfilled, complete, no pain or regret, in fact he didn't feel . . . anything. He sat up on the couch wondering how long he'd been there. Toddy noticed the silver case and instruments with the small pill box still lay on the table. His eye was drawn to a large black pistol lying on top of a handwritten note. The sight of the gun brought him to his senses and he picked up the little silver pill box first and checked it's contents, to his relief it still had some of the white powder in it.

"I'll leave that until later," he thought, placing the pill box back, he picked up the gun. The black pistol felt heavy in his hands but somehow right. He felt it's weight, bouncing it softly, getting used to the feeling of the dark wooden grip. He had never held a gun like this before. The feeling was a good one, a powerful electric tingling surge running through his fingers. Was it the stuff he smoked last night or the pistol? He couldn't differentiate between the two at the moment. The whole experience of yesterday was connecting him to a new way of living, his new future. Toddy picked up the note but knew what it said before he read it.

You know what to do. He knew what to do alright. He would have to pass this final test before he began his new life in London. He saw the whole thing as a quest. He talked to himself aloud.

"Get back to Brum, kill Eddie Fewtrell, get back to London. Simple stuff Toddy. Let's go!"

His voice sounded loud and confident in the silent, empty club. He stood up swaying slightly. He picked up the silver case and slid it into his jacket pocket. As he picked up the gun he caught a glimpse of himself in the Booth mirrors. He looked different somehow and he couldn't work out why but he liked what he saw. Smart, secret, deadly.

Hair Trigger

Chapter 14

Eddie's mind was elsewhere. He was working the Bermuda Club for all it was worth but he couldn't stop thinking about the new project. He was impatient to sell on the Bermuda to any mug that was willing to put their money into what he considered a sinking ship, although at that moment the ship was floating just fine. Plenty of cash was coming in, lots of new customers and fewer raids since the fight, helped no doubt by Dixie's tip offs, but something hung over the place for Eddie. Things could've so easily have gone the other way. If the Irish hadn't shown up that night and Don hadn't fired off a couple of shots into the ceiling he and his brothers would've been back on the streets of Aston scratching for a living. He felt he was on borrowed time. The new club was coming along very quickly, but not fast enough for the ever impatient Eddie.

The Cedar Club as it was now to be called, thanks to the purchase of Billy Smith's wood, which now lined almost every wall in the place giving it a Swiss style appearance was a fresh start, something legal. Eddie dared to hope it could be a spring board for other projects. All the licensing had been applied for and after a bit of bribing of the corrupt elements of Birmingham City Council, the go ahead for planning, drinks, and music licences were all approved.

Hazel had kicked off about the idea of the wood lined walls as she had spent months designing her plush red velvet, up market interior, but as Eddie constantly pointed out.

"A bargain's a bargain Bab."

After a while she just gave up arguing, muttering under her breath to anyone that would listen that the club looked like

"Britain's biggest fucking sauna," but Eddie knew he'd made the right decision buying the wood. The *bear* on the other hand *was* a mistake, although Eddie would never admit it as he never admitted anything that didn't go his way, saying instead that the bear would be the Cedar Club's mascot. The other brothers weren't too happy about having to clear up the constant trail of shit that always led a trail to the ever smelly Bear's, sleeping place. There was mutinous talk of shooting the animal and dumping him in the canal behind the club, but as Eddie never bothered himself with any shit clearing, and couldn't see the bother of the animal he would've strangled any would-be assassin. The brothers couldn't keep their feelings or their mutiny to themselves and, after a noisy confrontation, Eddie agreed to keep the bear with him in the Bermuda club until the Cedar club was finished.

The Bermuda kept on drawing crowds. The bear had made itself at home and was popular with the customers walking through the bar as if it were the most natural thing in the world. People even bought *Barnaby* drinks so the poor animal was pissed most of the time.

The Fewtrell's reputation went before them now and so the club started to attract the rougher types. People who wanted to associate with what they thought were gangsters, men *and* women who had, or were in the process of getting themselves a reputation. Fights had become commonplace and the light atmosphere of the early days had been replaced with one of a tinder box awaiting a small spark that would ignite a furnace of violence at any moment. Eddie had cut the staff to a minimum. Not through choice it must be said but because of the fight with the Market Mob only a few weeks before, staff had become a problem. Eddie found himself doing just about everything from glass collecting, meeting and greeting to serving beer at the bar. The younger brothers did what they could but he wanted the Cedar Club finished as soon as possible so he had split the family up in to two groups. One group in the Bermuda club and one getting the Cedar ready for it's opening night. Things were hectic but moving forward. The word had gone out that the Bermuda club was up for sale. A few dreamers had come forward offering to take the place on and go half on the profits with Fewtrell but these were dismissed immediately. Eventually a serious offer came in. Eddie was approached by an old associate called Jackie Diamond, a small time jewellery fence, selling dodgy diamonds with an even dodgier french accent. Born Jack Grimes in Dudley, Jackie changed his name by deed poll and his accent by watching 8 millimetre french porn films on his home projector. With the help of various gayly coloured cravats, he passed himself off as a burgundy viscount to unsuspecting punters, who couldn't spot the difference between a false French accent and a dodgy diamond. Jackie had decided to make Eddie an offer on the club. The offer was generous considering the club didn't even have a drinks license never mind a gambling one. Eddie wanted to snap Jackie's hand off but his Rag market habits kicked in driving the price of the club up to a ridiculous amount. Jackie started to back off so Eddie just began dropping the price until Jackie Diamond leant across the bar and held his hand out to close the deal. The price was still way above the first offer but Jackie felt he had a bargain. Eddie reached for Jackie's hand but the deal was never closed. At the moment of closure a tall man in a silver mohair suit brushed Jackie to one side, leaning across the bar, a black look in his eye.

"Are you Eddie Fewtrell?"

To all who saw him he seemed drunk but Toddy Burns had been enjoying his new found passion and the little pill box of heroin was nearly empty.

"Did you fucking hear me? Are you Eddie F . . . " without really looking who was asking, his mind still on the deal with Jackie Diamond, Eddie barked.

"YES, I'm fucking Eddie Fewtrell, what do you want?"

"I've come to complete my quest."

Toddy dug in the back of his trousers and pulled out the pistol.

"This is a little message from the Krays!" and he brought the gun up aiming it at Eddie's head. Jackie sprang forward knocking Toddy's arm. The gun went off with a deafening bang even surprising Toddy. His ears rang with a high pitched tone. The shock made his head swim as his adrenalin joined the heroin in his bloodstream and the room began to spin around him. The bullet had grazed Eddie, tearing a small strip from his shirt under his arm and gone on to lodge itself in the wooden bar behind him. Toddy pulled himself back to the present. Jackie had turned and run into the club shouting,

"Gun!" at the top of his voice. Eddie was still trapped behind the bar. Toddy climbed clumsily over the bar and this time Toddy brought the pistol up in front of him, his eye looking straight down the barrel of the gun as he brought the sights down on his prey. Eddie backed away, hands in front of his face in useless protection. They stood there like that for a few seconds. Toddy's mind had started to wander again. He had smoked plenty of the foul smelling substance before coming into the club for some Dutch courage. But now the heroin was slowing him down. Making every second stop as if it were a film speeding up then slowing down frame by frame. Eddie saw his chance and picking up a vodka bottle flung it at his assailant. The bottle found it's mark smashing into Toddy's face. The glass didn't harm Toddy but he dropped the gun on the bar floor, rubbing at the stinging alcohol in his eyes he was blinded for a second. Eddie grabbed the gun and it was at this moment that Eddie finally recognised the gunman.

"It's you, you fucking murdering bastard. You killed Micky Higgins and wrecked my club and now you're working for the fucking KRAYS!"

The punters in the club began to scatter to whatever hiding places they could find, under the roulette tables or hiding behind upturned furniture sending the glasses smashing to the ground, adding to the chaos. Eddie half pointing the gun in Toddy general direction felt the kick as the gun fired again. Toddy leapt towards

Eddie trying to out pace him, reaching for his gun. BANG! The thing had a life of it's own. BANG! Off it went again, only this time Toddy's ear exploded, showering the bar with bright red blood. Toddy felt no pain. Just the punch from the bullet spinning him around, unbalancing him. The customers that could see only saw the man twist and fall in the middle of a thick blood red mist. BANG! The gun kept firing followed by the smash of glass as the bullets found their home in the mirrored walls around the club. The trigger had been filed down so much that the firing pin kept being activated by the slightest touch which in turn, sent the thirteen brass cartridges contained in the clip into the barrel one by one. Eddie held onto the gun, jumping from the shock every time it went off. In the end he just pointed it at the ceiling and hoped for the best.

Toddy knelt down on all fours his head becoming clearer. He could see the blood spraying out of his head onto the floor of the bar all around him forming bright red fountains. At first Toddy froze when he saw the beauty of the fountains unable to comprehend that the red spray was blood or that it was coming from his head. The image took him back to the night when he watched his blood pour into the snow at the doors of the Market Tavern. That seemed like a long time ago now, his old life. There was no pain at all thanks to the heroin. He knew something bad had happened but didn't feel scared or panicked. Toddy didn't feel anything, just that contented feeling he had found in London a few days before. He pulled himself off the floor, grabbing at the hole where his ear had been. He stumbled from behind the bar and made for the front door joining in the confusion as the punters who by now were streaming out of the club and collecting in small groups in the cold street. He could feel the warm blood gushing out from his head, trickling down his neck, soaking him. Toddy pushed past people, men swearing as he did and women screaming at the sight of his blood.

The groups of people began to talk amongst themselves about how Eddie Fewtrell had shot a man in the head and there had been a gunfight between him and the Krays, mistaking the hair triggered single gun for many. Another rumour about the Fewtrells had started and the incident wasn't even two minutes old.

Toddy stumbled on down Navigation Hill, turning into a doorway to hide the blood soaked suit as two police cars and a Paddy wagon drove by, blue lights flashing and bells ringing. Automatically he continued down the street towards his flat, no emotion just survival. He'd be safe there for a while but he'd have to get out of Birmingham now. His life wasn't worth shit in this town anymore. The loss of blood had brought on the sinking feeling again as the heroin began to wear off. He would have to go back to the Krays for more.

"Maybe they'll give him another gun so he could finish the job," he fantasied.

The police arrived within fifteen minutes. Dixie was in the lead car. As he pulled up members of the crowd came forward to say there had been a gunfight between the Fewtrells and the Krays and that someone was dead. Dixie expected the worst but ordered his men to keep the growing group of customers and sight seers away from the club door. He entered gun in hand. Eddie and Jackie Diamond were the only two left in the club now. The ammunition in the hair triggered pistol had run out and it was lying on the bar. The two men were bent over a body lying against a wall, a growing pool of blood surrounding it. The club was dark but Dixie could see the figure was clearly dead.

Eddie jumped when he saw Dixie approach.

"Have they all gone?" Dixie enquired.

"He's dead." Eddie replied grey faced.

"Who's dead? Who is it?" expecting the name of one of the Fewtrell brothers.

"Barnaby. He's dead."

"Barnaby, is he one of your lot?" Dixie couldn't place the name. Jackie rose from the body.

"He *is* a fucking bear you twat." his French accent beginning to slip. Dixie stared harder through the dim light and now he could see the small bear in a waistcoat and neckerchief. A blue trilby lay on the floor besides the body, confused Dixie turned to Jackie.

"He's a fucking dead bear now mate," he said sarcastically, relieved it wasn't a human lying on the floor. Eddie was gutted. For the first time Dixie saw real anguish in Eddie's eyes. "Who did it? Was it the Krays? I fucking told you they'd be back. Fancy shooting a bear though. I mean that's fucking low ain't it." Dixie shook his head feigning sorrow, Jackie Diamond stopped him,

"No it was Eddie who . . . " Eddie jumped into the conversation quickly.

"It was me who scared em off." Eddie gave Jackie a dark stare. The last thing he needed now was people to hear that he'd shot his own pet bear with one of his stray shots. He'd never live it down, better to let the Krays take the blame.

"Anyway thank god it was just the bear and not one of the punters." Eddie shot a sideways glance at Jackie hiding his rarely seen emotions.

"Just one thing lads." Dixie said, "What the fuck is a bear doing in your club? I hope he was a member or you'll be in big trouble." The three men laughed but without any real conviction. Dixie left the room and came back with a large black canvas bag. The three men lifted the bear into the bag then Dixie went outside again returning shortly with two uniformed officers. They picked up the bag by its canvas strops at each end and clumsily carried the body out to the waiting ambulance. Dixie turned to Eddie. "You've got to shut the club. This is getting out of hand." Eddie agreed.

As the police men carried the black body bag into the street a murmur rose from the large crowd.

"Eddie Fewtrell killed one of the Kray gang." The voices began to grow in volume.

"Shot him in the head. I saw it happen." The gossip had begun to work it's way around the grapevine and within an hour people had heard about it on the other side of the city and the body was still warm in it's bag. Of course either Eddie, Dixie or Jackie Diamond didn't try to dispel the false rumours, although Jackie suddenly had second thoughts about going into the night club business, deciding to stick instead to fencing jewellery.

Dixie cleared the bear's body with his bosses and the remains were destroyed without any investigation. Dixie pointed out to the chief of police that they had no control over the underworld of Birmingham, even though they would like to think they had. If the people of the second city wanted to believe that Eddie Fewtrell had killed a Kray gang member, then that would at least send out the message to local criminals that there was one gang in Birmingham you didn't cross.

The day after the shooting the Birmingham Evening Mail headlines were about how the city was about to become the *Gangland Capital of Great Britain.* The story told of a death contract being taken out by the Krays on Eddie Fewtrell. The story was a total fabrication, written by a local, inexperienced corespondent but without realising it, The Evening Mail had hit the nail on the head. Everyone in the city began to get pulled into the story and one by one various gangs, families, the IRA, even the police offered to help the Fewtrells keep the Krays out of the city. No one bothered to ask the Fewtrells if all the rumours were true, all *they* wanted to do was make a living, not get into a war with one of the most vicious gangs in the country. Unfortunately for them though, things were moving faster now and taking on a life of their own, spiralling towards a point somewhere in the not too distant future where the outcome was still uncertain.

A week after the incident Eddie was summoned to meet the chief of police. Dixie accompanied Eddie and the meeting took place away from the station at an Italian restaurant on the Hagley Road. When Eddie arrived he was surprised to see several of the top police men sitting around a circular table chatting. As he approached the table the men stood up and greeted him. Dixie introduced him one by one. Eddie felt out of his depth suddenly but was pleasantly surprised by their welcome. The chief took over the meeting.

"I supposed you're wondering why we've asked you here tonight?" Eddie nodded expecting something would be said about shutting down the Bermuda club or stopping the licence on the Cedar Club.

"Well we . . . the Birmingham police force . . . he let the words hang in the air "would like to say thank you for keeping the Krays out of Birmingham." He continued. "And . . . we are here to help in anyway we can." The chief plonked his wine glass on the table and Eddie could see that they had all been here drinking and chatting well before he arrived.

"Eh . . . Hold on a minute. I ain't trying to stop anyone getting in anywhere. All I'm trying to do is make a living for me and my brothers." Eddie thought he'd put a stop to this whole thing straightaway. The men began talking under their breath to one another. Eddie couldn't make out the words but got the general feeling that he was about to be stitched up. The chief took over again.

"Well Mr Fewtrell whether you like it or not and whatever your reasons for your battle with the Kray twins. You and your brothers are on the front line of a war for this great city." He stopped and took a sip of wine. "Now, although we can't obviously get involved in any illegal situations. We *can* help you in anyway possible *within the limits of the law* to keep your clubs open, in return for things to be kept running smoothly in the city. Any cooperation in this would certainly put you in good stead with the Birmingham licensing committee and I'm sure you could open as many clubs as you like if the arrangement we make tonight is adhered to. Your refusal to help, on the other hand could make things very difficult for you and your family." Eddie was dumbstruck. These bastards were just as bad as the fucking Krays. "I'm sorry . . . what are you saying.?"

"Oh I think I've made myself very clear Edward. You keep the Krays out and we'll grant you freedom of the city so to speak. If you don't then you'll regret it. There, is that clearer?" one or two of the men began to snigger.

"They've fucking done me like a kipper." Eddie thought. He gave a glance at Dixie. "Cheers mate," he said sarcastically. Dixie turned to the men.

"Sir, may I make a suggestion?" The chief nodded.

"Well if Mr Fewtrell is to keep out the Krays or anyone else out that wants to get a foothold here in Birmingham. Then maybe we could provide him with written permission from your office to be able to protect himself, as we can't offer him any protection against the London underworld. Maybe give him a licence to carry a gun or something to protect himself with. Also it might be worth passing on any information we hear from our men in London about the Krays' movements?"

The circle of men began to confer secretly to each other. Dixie smiled at Eddie and gave a shrug of his shoulders. Eddie sat there with the feeling that the meeting was spinning out of control. He'd had enough of this nonsense.

"Hold on you lot. Did it ever occur to any of you that I don't want a fucking gun? I don't need one. That's not how this is gonna play out. We've given em a scare they wont be back. I'm not gonna be drawn into a war with anyone. I'm gonna run my clubs keep me head down and make a few quid. That's all I'm doing. So just forget any talk of guns." The policemen sat in silence for a second then continued to chat quietly.

"I'm talking to my fucking self here." Eddie tuned to Dixie exasperated.

"I'm afraid it's gone well beyond that now Mr Fewtrell." The chief brought the meeting back to order.

"Please call me Eddie. Everyone calls me Eddie." he pleaded.
"Well Eddie . . . you don't seem to realise how dangerous these bastards are. Whether you like it or not you're in the middle of this shit storm now sonny. If we let just one of those Cockney fucks get a foot hold in this town you're going to be fucked and we're going to be fucked, and Her Majesty's Police force don't like to be fucked, we like to *do* the fucking." The police chief began to get animated. He continued, "so I suggest you get your head around the idea and get your shit together because this is just the beginning. They will come back and this time you might not be so lucky. The body in the bag might be you or one of your brothers!"

"Unless you have anymore bears that would like to take a bullet for you." One of the other men finished off the chief's sentence. The circle cracked up into hysterical laughter.

"I'm glad you find this so funny . . . I was very close to that bear," He turned to Dixie, "I thought we said to keep the bear thing *quiet"* Eddie stared at Dixie. "I don't like being taken the piss out of."

"Come on Eddie it's funny. I mean it's like a bloody goon show sketch." The chief was smiling now.

"Look we're on your side. I understand you have to bend the rules a bit, we all do but if you do this thing for us we can make your life very easy in this city. We'll stop anyone moving into compete with you, at least until your on your feet with your new club, oh and Dixon is right. You do need the type of protection we can't provide, so get yourself a gun. I wouldn't go for a pistol though too easy to trace.

What do you suggest gentlemen?"

The other men all nodded agreement offering various solutions. Dixie stepped forward.

"Shotgun sir. Sawn off shotgun." The chief looked around the other officers.

"See I told you he was good. He's going to do very well for himself that lad." The other men looked at Dixie smiling and nodding approval.

"You cant trace a shot gun sir." Dixie added.

"We'll there you have it Eddie. Get a shotgun and saw the barrel and stock off. That should sort them out if they come for you. If anything happens we'll write it off as self-defence. You know . . . to a point we can cover your arse. Don't kill any women and children though . . . Or bears."

The officers exploded in laughter once more.

"If things go well Eddie I may introduce you to our lodge. Show Eddie the door now Dixon. I'm sure he's a busy man and those clubs don't run themselves."

The room fell quiet. Eddie suddenly felt very unwelcome. Ed stood up not knowing whether to thank them or tell them to go to hell. After a short silence he thanked them and left. Dixie accompanied him to the door.

"Lodge?" Eddie said "What the fuck's he taking about?"

"Freemasons Ed." Dixie couldn't believe Eddie didn't know what he meant.

"Most of the Police force are Freemasons, surely you knew that right?"

Eddie nodded still none the wiser.

"I gotta get back. Cheers Dixie I know your trying to help me. I do appreciate it mate," with that he was gone.

Dixie returned to the table. The chief had started to talk about the Fewtrells again.

"He's a sharp lad that Eddie, could be good for us. It's always good to have someone who's willing to do a bit of dirty work for you. Stops us getting our hands grubby if you know what I mean." The other men agreed. "We'll keep him on a short rope though. Don't let them have too much freedom. That way if the shit hits the fan we've always got him where we need him. Every now and then we'll get the uniforms to raid his clubs. Keep him on his toes. Then we can step in and make it look like we're the ones who've got him off the hook. Trust me gentlemen he'll be very grateful and if things get out of hand, if the wrong person gets shot, he'll take the drop, not us. This is all working out better than I ever thought it would. Well done Dixon." Dixie raised his glass.

"There's one born every minute sir."

Final Hit

Chapter 15

Months passed before Toddy Burns was found. His estranged wife was the one to make the gruesome discovery, with no contact from her husband she had finally plucked up the courage to head back to their flat and collect her things. She found him in the living room in the centre of a huge pool of his own dried blood and a pungent stench of death. After the shooting at the Bermuda Toddy had managed to get home. He did his best to stop the bleeding and although he wasn't too happy about losing his ear from the stray bullet he thought the Krays would appreciate the scar and still offer him the job. At least he had tried to kill Eddie Fewtrell and the lack of a left ear proved it. His suit was ruined but he could get another when he got back to London. That's what it was all about now, getting back to London where he belonged. The blood had started to clot and slow now. He had lost a fair bit and he was amazed at how much an ear could bleed. He cleaned himself up as best he could then wrapping a towel around his head and putting on a clean white shirt and his old black suit. Toddy began packing in earnest. After half an hour he slumped back into his armchair, exhausted. The lack of blood was bad enough, making him fatigued and dizzy but the lack of heroin in his now depleted bloodstream had brought on cold sweats and shivers. He had a craving for it like he'd never had before. The silver case lay on the table in front of him. He controlled the feeling and slowly, carefully opened the little case and picked up the pill box from within. This time though instead of taking the tiny spoon from inside he picked up the syringe. After preparing the heroin he pulled the brown liquid into the needle. The tiny syringe felt almost as powerful as the gun had a few hours before. Toddy waited a second, staring at the instrument before stabbing it into a chosen vein on the inside of his elbow. The hit was instant and massive. The feeling of euphoria racing though every vein and artery, flowing to the extremities of his body, leaving him motionless. The heroin relaxed Toddy to the point he was hardly conscious. The drug also stopped his blood from clotting so his ear, or what was now just a hole in the side of his head began to bleed again. As he slumped there in his favourite chair, his life blood slowly trickled from him until there simply wasn't enough to sustain him any more. Toddy slumbered and dreamt about swinging London, fast cars, money, success, contentment, all just a train ride away. He'd finally made something of himself. His last thought on this earth was that he'd made it. He was really somebody. Softly unnoticed, his heart slowed then finally stopped, what little blood there was left in him soaked into the cheap material of his armchair and natty old suit. His final resting place a dirty, run down old flat on the outskirts of Birmingham, filled with cheap furniture and the smell of rotting food. Outside the net curtained windows, the never ending noise of the city continued. Nobody would miss him. No one would mourn him and that was the end of Toddy Burns.

Real Killers

Chapter 16

"Facking liability!"

Ronnie Kray couldn't believe how stupid this made him and his brother look.

"What were we facking thinking sending that northern monkey to do our work?"

Weeks had passed before the word about the failed attempt on Eddie Fewtrell's life had found it's way to the East End of London.

"If he shows up here again in his poncy suit I'll skin him alive. I mean how can you go to shoot someone and end up getting shot yourself . . . With *your own facking gun for fack's sake.*" Ronnie had gone into one of his tantrums, Reggie knew them all too well. They started off like this and ended up in a club somewhere with Ronnie giving some innocent bloke a Chelsea smile.

"Calm down bruv. We ain't lost anything ave we. I mean he'll be back, looking for more of the heroin, when he shows up . . . " Reggie stopped mid-sentence looking for the right words, in the end deciding to go with what he originally thought, even if it upset his fragile stated brother. "You can have your fun with him. He's a nobody. You're a somebody now, so facking act like one. We are the KRAYS!" He almost shouted the words. Ronnie exploded.

"Yes we're the facking Krays but that ain't gonna mean fack all if the word gets back to the Americans that we can't even handle a hit on some yokel from Birmingham. Never mind what the other gangs around here will think. Have you heard some of the things the being said about us? How we're losing our grip. People are taking the piss Reg, I cant have it. We ain't nothing without respect and people respect fear." Reg spoke with a smooth calm cold voice.

"People *do* fear us. We can't let em see you acting like this over facking nothing. They *will* think we've lost it."

The brothers sat in silence for a while Ronnie stewing, working himself into one of his black moods and Reggie trying to calm the situation until finally Reg spoke.

"We'll get some proper people in to do the job. *Real* killers. We should've asked them to do it in the first place." Ronnie suddenly perked up.

"The Lambrianous brothers?"

Chris and Tony Lambrianous had been childhood friends with the Krays; incredibly loyal, they were employed by the Firm to enforce the enforcers. They weren't particularly hard men, although both were good fighters, but they were vicious and organised, willing to go that extra step to get the result they wanted. That's what Ronnie and Reg liked about them.They didn't need to prove themselves. They had metered out plenty of punishment to anyone that stepped out of line in the Kray's empire, taking things to extremes and disposing of the evidence without needing to be told very tidy, very professional was how Ronnie liked to describe them.

The Lambrianous were summoned to a meeting the next day. Both handsome lads of Italian decent and a far bit younger than the Krays they were classed as family and looked up to Ronnie and Reg with a certain amount of awe. The Lambrianous were treated with respect by the outer circle of wannabes coming and going around the Krays.

"Ron and Reg told the brothers everything about the deal with the yanks; the move into Birmingham and the heroin. They were both sworn to secrecy. Drugs like heroin weren't the type of things even the Krays wanted to be associated with. They had told the Americans their plans and now had to be seen to be following them through.

"The city is just lying there waiting to be opened up like an oyster." Ronnie said, pleased with his description, selling it to the Lambrianous. Reg backed up Ron,

"There's nothing stopping us, just some local family called The Fewtrells. They got the monopoly on the clubs in the town and we need the clubs to sell the heroin and the Fewtrells won't play ball. We've put the feelers out and it could be a fucking gold mine" Reg continued. "The main brother is called Eddie Fewtrell. He's the one that insulted us. He's gotta go." Ron had moved over to the large glass tank that held his precious collection of snakes. He picked one up and let it coil through his hands, enjoying it's smooth skin against his palms, "families are like snakes," the other men looked at Ron, eyebrows raised waiting for the comparison to be completed, "it's only the head that's dangerous, cut off the head and the rest is just tail. That's what you two have to do here. Cut off the head of the family. Once that's done the rest will just fold. Kill Eddie facking Fewtrell!" He almost spat the words. "I'm sick of his facking name. Do it so everyone knows it's the Krays. We gotta let them fackers know we mean business and boys . . . *Don't fack it up* . . . People are watching." The meeting continued with Ronnie's contribution floating between ridiculous comparisons and aggressive, embarrassing rants. Ronnie's mood swings hadn't gone unnoticed by many of the London underworld. Paranoid delusions had started to creep into his mind over the past few months, most of them having no real basis but who could he trust, if not the Lambrianous brothers?

Ronnie gave the Lambrianous his gleaming gun metal Jaguar to use for the weekend, it's boot loaded with anything they could think of that might come in handy for the hit: a large axe, shovels, hammers, duct tape, a saw, even a thick canvas body bag Tony Lambrianous had stolen from an ambulance, and *most importantly* two new loaded black Beretta pistols complete with four inch long silencers. They also took a case of money, £2000, just in case they needed to pay off any locals for information on the Fewtrells' movements and whereabouts. The brothers always dressed smart, handsome and cool they had no problem pulling the ladies wherever they went and this little jaunt to Birmingham was going to be no exception. The M1 motorway was empty and Chris enjoyed escaping the constrictions of the London traffic and putting his foot down on the throttle he opened up the Jag's engine. The sudden acceleration pushed them back into their thick red leather seats. The roar of the V8 engine settling into a soft purr as the car began to cruise at 80MPH the unfamiliar countryside whizzing by their windows. Tony Lambrianou settled back into the car's luxury and lit a cigarette staring out the window feeling like a fish out of water. His brother tried to comfort his obvious insecurity about leaving London for the first time.

"A bit of business, a bit of fun, in that order." Chris Lambrianou lectured his younger brother. Tony didn't acknowledge his words. Just continued to stare out the window, deep in thought. Chris pressed him.

"Penny for your thoughts bruv." Tony spoke without turning or breaking his gaze.

"Maybe we could make our own mark on the city?" Tony offered. "Get our own club instead of hanging on Ron and Reg's shirt tails all the time."

Chris didn't like his younger brothers independent streak,

"Let's not go over this again Anthony, the Krays are our brothers, near enough anyway. I won't have any talk about going out on our own right now. Ron and Reg have been good to us and you're saying we should repay it by fucking them off and setting up on our own, that's not how we were brought up is it?" Tony shook his head feeling guilty.

"They ain't gonna last forever though are they. I mean you heard Ron the other day at the meeting. What the fuck was he talking about? Comparing everything to his bloody snakes, weird."

"Listen little bruv," Chris reached across the car, keeping one hand on the steering wheel of the speeding car and patting his other on his brother's shoulder. "that's dangerous talk. I've seen blokes get a hiding for lesser talk than that. Keep your thoughts to yourself. There's plenty of time to go it alone. Let's do the job and get back home eh. Maybe pick up a couple of Brummie birds along the way."

The Car floated along the empty motorway. The Sunday morning traffic was minimal. Anthony began to relax and the conversation turned to football, boxing cars and clothes, until the Birmingham city signs appeared bringing them back to the business in hand. They pulled off the slip road leading them through Aston and the scruffy suburbs, to the city centre where they were met by two of Tom Shellby's men at the same hotel the Krays had used a short time before.

"How you doing lads?" Shellby's man held his hand out welcoming the brothers with his friendly Birmingham accent. The Lambrianous just nodded arrogantly ignoring the handshake. Both brothers got out the car eyeing up the two waiting Brummies.

"Welcome to Birmingham. How was the drive lads?" Shellby's man tried to break the ice again.

"Never mind that shit." Chris Lambrianous said aggressively.

"We ain't here to make friends mate, quite the opposite. We need to get started on this today. I wanna be out of this shit-hole of a city as soon as. Now, we'll check in to the hotel, whilst we're doing that you find us someone that's close to the Fewtrells n*ot* family, a friend, someone that's open to earning a bit of cash and wouldn't mind working with Ron and Reggie Kray. We need information about Eddie Fewtrell. We are going to visit the Fewtrells tonight, nice and subtle, we are just punters out for a drink tonight gentlemen. We wanna suss the situation out then we'll do the job either last thing tonight or first thing tomorrow morning. By the time the Old Bill get a sniff we'll be back in the smoke bruv." Chris smiled at his silent sterner faced brother. Anthony just nodded, a cold look in his eye. The men went there separate ways without another word, Shellby's men biting their lips and racking their brains as to who knew the Fewtrells well enough to inform on them.

Mod Night.

Chapter 17

The Cedar Club had been open for three weeks. The club was an instant hit. Birmingham had never really had anything like it before, bringing top bands and singers to the city. It was, for many, the first time they had had the opportunity to see many of the acts that were now regular performers on the Friday night TV show Ready Steady Go! The plush cedar wood lined interior gave the club a European feel, something that was very fashionable and unobtainable for many working class folk.

Hazel Fewtrell had taken control of the bookings as she had her ear to the ground on the British music scene. Local bands were used to fill the gaps in-between finding major crowd pullers, but Sunday nights were always hard to fill. Eddie had come up with the idea of a Mod night after reading in the Sunday papers about the Mods and Rocker riots in Margate and Brighton during last bank holiday. The young Mods had nowhere to go to dance to the black American soul music and R&B that was flooding over the Atlantic and the many home grown mod bands, that were always on the verge of breaking big.

"They're all dressed up and nowhere to go." Eddie had a way of stating the obvious but in this case he was right on the button, and now Sunday nights had become very busy. The doors opened at seven o'clock but by six large groups of smartly dressed young peacocks began to arrive on brightly painted chrome covered scooters in clouds of purple two-stroke oil. They hung around outside the club, checking each other out, their scooters lining the pavement outside the club all the way down the street, chrome and paint sparkling in the street lights.

The night drew Mod gangs from all over the city. Some in pea green parkas with huge, wolf fur trimmed hoods protecting the immaculate shiny mohair suits that the Mods wore underneath. The girls in the latest styles of hipsters, pencil or miniskirts, long boots and bob hair cuts perched precariously, sitting side saddle on the pillion seats of the chrome covered machines, doing their very best to look cosmopolitan.

The buzz in the club was almost palatable. The thick groove of the soul and R&B pumped through the dance floor driving the young dancers, making shapes and copying the moves they'd seen on TV shows that weekend. The coolest faces stood at the bar, looking good, drinking vodka and tonic or some other short, never a pint as that would be far too working class. They spent their time chatting and blowing clouds of cigarette smoke into the flashing lights above the dance floor. Uninterested in the girls, they were there to be seen and adored by the lesser Mods.

Don and Chrissy chatted to the heads of the various Mod gangs, being bought drinks, making small talk, acting important. Eddie always took Hazel out on Sundays so Don was in charge with Chrissy as back up. Don liked to let everyone know who he was, strutting around the club smartly dressed his blonde quiff standing high on his head and acting the Al Capone.

Whenever there was trouble he and Chrissy would step in and turf the ruffians out, maybe Chrissy would give an odd slap or two just to show them the Fewtrell's were in charge, but nothing too heavy. If things really kicked off then the dedicated doormen stepped in to help. Big lads all, hard as nails and happy to fight anyone, semi-professional wrestlers, bare knuckle boxers, body builders and the like, all in smart black suits and white shirts bought by Hazel, they made up the security, giving the place an air of exclusivity. There was rarely any trouble on a Sunday. A mohair suit was two weeks wages and far too much an investment in cool to be ruined by a scuffle with some ticket from the sticks.

Across town the Lambrianous brothers were waiting at the foyer of the hotel for the return of Shellby's men. They had been having a hard time tracking down someone close to the Fewtrells. After spending Sunday afternoon trawling the bars and pubs of Birmingham they eventually caught up with Jackie Diamond at a little bar in at the back of town called The Twisted Wheel. One of them stayed with Jackie and the other went to fetch the Lambrianous.

Jackie had been lying low after the shooting. Eddie had continued to press him into buying the Bermuda club, becoming very heavy when Jackie still refused to purchase the place. Eddie had changed since the Cedar club had opened. He began to flex his muscle around the city a bit, handing out the odd beating here and there, pushing the other hard families out of the town centre into the suburbs, showing everyone who the boss and carrying a sawn off shooter under his rain coat whenever he left the club to get in his car. He was paranoid but on the up. Jackie preferred the former Eddie Fewtrell, but that didn't mean he would spill the beans about Eddie to anyone that asked, especially these Cockneys. He had an inkling who they were working for but tried to put a brave face on. The Lambrianous didn't think much of The Twisted Wheel. They crowded around Jackie, Chris Lambrianou being friendly buying, drinks for the five of them. Anthony didn't even bother to hide the reason why they were there, almost snarling at Jackie,

"Where the fack is that accent from then? Cardiff? Anthony was finding it hard to hide his aggression. Jackie Diamond tried his best to continue with his French facade but the situation was starting to dawn on him that this was going to get dodgy. "Well fack me if it ain't Pepe Le Pew." Shellby's men laughed along with Chris's vulgar jokes aimed at Jackie's accent and the barmaids breasts. Jackie faked a smile, but knew what was coming, that hollow feeling in his gut slowly filling with dread.

The questions they were asking about the Fewtrells were childish to say the least. No real information was gained they were just going through the motions until it reached a point were they could give Jackie Diamond a good beating. He knew it, they knew it and they knew he knew it. It was all about making a point to everyone in Birmingham that the Krays were coming and anyone who knew, or mixed with the Fewtrells was in the firing line.

The only real information that was gleamed by grilling Jackie was, 1.) Eddie Fewtrell owned the Cedar club and 2.) He was always there.

Anyone could have told you the first was true, but the latter was false because tonight was a Sunday and Jackie Diamond knew Eddie *never* worked Sundays, but he wasn't gonna tell these bastards.

After several rounds of drinks were bought and thrown back, Jackie reluctantly followed the Lambrianous brothers outside the Club to a small yard that backed onto an old warehouse. The club used the area as a storage space for the empty aluminium barrels of beer and wooden crated empty bottles that stacked several feet up the walls either side of the yard. It stank of the sweet, putrid smell of gone off beer and rat's piss.

If you were a fly on the wall you'd think you were watching a scene from a Second World War movie, with a prisoner being taken out to execution, two men in front, two behind and the prisoner in the middle, head down in acceptance for the brutal fate that was only moments away. There was the usual speeches. The Londoners had heard it all before.

"Come on lads there's no need for this," Jackie pleaded "I've told you everything I know. What's the point in giving me a kicking for nothing. I could be a good friend to you lads if you're making moves into Birmingham." His French accent replaced by the black country one he was born with. Anthony Lambrianou sniggered.

"Do we look like we need a second class fence for a friend? No mate you'll be better of to us dead."

It was at that point Jackie realised just how deep in he was. He was about to become a sacrificial lamb to the name of the Krays. The Lambrianous took a back seat on the beating to start with. Shellby's men stepped in for the initial roughing up. A few slaps here and there, degrading Jackie step by step, asking pointless questions again and again. When Jackie replied they just slapped him hard across the jaw. Disorientation, anger, rage, helplessness, mercy pleading, then the golden glint of brass as the knuckle duster destroyed his nose. WHAM! A thousand fireworks went off in Jackie Diamond's head. BAM! Again the brass glint flew past his eyes, this time shattering his jaw. Jackie looked up at his assailant and saw a smiling Anthony Lambrianous standing over him. Jackie lay there taking in Anthony's handsome but mean face, the sound of conversations in the distance, the smell of beer on the cold rippled concrete. Jackie felt someone pull his hair back sharply, the action brought him back to his senses. He wished it hadn't. The cold steel blade slid easily across his throat. He breathed but nothing happened. Normal reactions were gone, replaced by a drowning breathlessness and the bubbling sound of blood leaking from his throat. Jackie grabbed his open neck, eyes wide in panic. The Lambrianous and Shellby's men were laughing at him. He heard the metal gate slam against the bolts as the men left the yard. He'd been left for dead.

Before Jackie became French, when his name was still Jack Grimes, Jackie had an affliction. Something he'd suffered with his whole life, very low blood pressure, and on this day it was to be his saviour. When he had been a scampering child he had always hated the way the other boys had the energy to play full-tilt all day when he would feel faint at the slightest bit of mischief. The initial burst of blood slowed down enough for Jackie to drag himself one hand on his wound out onto the street only a few yards away. He lay there in a pool of his own blood for nearly an hour before a good samaritan could pluck up the courage to get involved by phoning an ambulance from the red call box, before disappearing into the neighbouring housing estate.

He regained consciousness two hours later. The stiff cold clean sheets of the hospital ward and the whiteness of the room gave it a dreamy feel. The police were talking to a doctor. Jackie tried to talk but a jagged pain shot through his neck and he remembered why he was there. The policeman turned to Jackie and leant over him about to ask the first of many questions. Jackie grabbed at the pencil and note pad sticking out of the officer's jacket pocket. He quickly scribbled *Dixie* on the pad and showed it to the policeman. At first the uniform tried to brush it aside but Jackie pushed the pad and name into his face, jabbing the scrawl with the pencil. The officer turned and left the room asking the doctor for a phone as he passed. The whiteness of the room slowly blurred into blackness as the exertion of his communication took its toll.

When he awoke Dixie was sat beside him in a chair, pencil and pad in hand. Jackie took in the surroundings again and nodding at Dixie he gestured for the pencil and pad.

They're going to kill Eddie tonight!

"Who's gonna kill Eddie?" Dixie sat up suddenly. *Cockneys.*

"Were they with the Krays . . . are the Krays in Birmingham Jackie?" *Killing Eddie Cedar club!! NOW!*

Dixie dropped the pad and without looking at Jackie he left the room. Jackie Diamond fell back in his bed and floated into the peaceful blackness once more.

The Cedar club resembled a beehive by the time the Lambrianous arrived. The dark grey Jaguar pulled up almost silently across the street from the club. All four men sat silently watching the comings and goings of the hundreds of Mod scooters buzzing along the road, chrome sparkling in the street lights. Chris Lambrianous got out of the rear passenger side door and took the two Beretta pistols from the car boot, he checked the contents and ran his hands over the bag with the cash in it. He couldn't help the thinking about running off into the night with that amount of cash, he could set himself up for life. Chris pushed the thought back into the far recesses of his mind. He got back inside the car and he handed one of the guns to his brother and both men screwed on the silencers to the black barrels. They began their vigil again. Shellby's men sat in the front of the car, the idea of having two of England's most notorious hit men sat behind them with loaded silenced pistols can't have been lost on them.

"There." Anthony leant forward tapping the man in front on the shoulder. "That's him isn't it." He pointed at the tall blonde man who had just stepped out of club's doorway. "Eddie Fewtrell?" Shellby's man couldn't say for sure.

"I think so. Can't tell from here."

"What's the point in you being here?" Chris said pushing the man's head forward. "Facking useless." Shellby's man tried to defend himself.

"What was that for? I don't know if it's him or not. I didn't say I fucking knew him did I? All I know is he's tall and blonde so that *must* be him. He certainly looks like he owns the place don't he?"Anthony leaned across the front seat and whispered in the man's ear.

"We'll I don't wanna walk over there and shoot the wrong facking bloke do I you silly cunt."

"Is that how your gonna do it, just walk up and bang?" The man in the driver's seat butted in. Chris Lambrianou spoke in a kinder voice, explaining.

"We wait for our moment then we both walk over there, Tony will do the main shot and I'll pop anyone that gets too nosey. Then we walk back here and you drive us away."

"What about the car? Someone will get the number plate." Shellby's man asked, panic in his voice.

"Already changed the plates before you picked us up from the hotel." Chris said smugly.

They sat back and continued to watch the tall blonde man strutting around the club's entrance, shaking hands and patting backs. Anthony Lambrianous smiled to himself. The tingling nerves ran through his fingertips as he fondled the gun. Ronnie Krays words ran through his mind. *Don't fuck it up!*

Eddie and Hazel Fewtrell sat facing each other in the little Italian candle lit restaurant owned by their friend Gigi. Eddie wasn't the most romantic of men but he was very generous when he had the cash. He had lavished Hazel with new jewellery and clothes since the new club had opened trying to make her happy. She had insisted they had one night together a week for the sake of their relationship. What was the point in making all this cash if you didn't get to show it off every now and again?

Eddie never really felt comfortable in these situations, Hazel had a tendency to ask too many questions. The attention the new club brought to Eddie had fuelled her already growing suspicions that he was screwing one or more of the pretty barmaids and she couldn't help herself probing.

Cash, pretty barmaids, fights, all the stuff he was busy trying to keep hidden from Hazel by slowly distancing her from the club and the business. On evenings such as this he always arranged other couples or friends to *accidentally* bump into Hazel and himself as it helped to break up the evening and more importantly, keep her chatting with her friends instead of asking those awkward questions. It also allowed Eddie to do a bit of wheeling and dealing with whomever had been invited. Hazel pretended not to catch on to Eddie's little arrangements, preferring instead to leave Eddie thinking he'd pulled the wool over her eyes. Anyway it gave her a chance to show off her latest fashion purchases.

Gigi's restaurant was a small affair with a basic menu of home cooked Italian food, but in a city which had virtually no choice in foreign food, Gigi's was seen as a positively exotic destination for a meal and it soon caught on with the up and coming of Birmingham. Eddie always sat facing the door wherever he was, an old habit, one eye on Hazel, one on the door.

"You never know when it's coming" he would say. At first Hazel thought he was being over dramatic, but lately she was more understanding about Eddie's paranoia.

Every time the door of the restaurant opened he would light up, expecting one of his incognito friends to step through the little glass panelled doorway.

"I've found an act from London I think we should have in the club." Hazel was asking permission, more than making a statement. She always did this, as in the end Eddie would believe he came up with the idea himself.

"He's gonna be big and we should get him before he gets on the telly. His agent said he's gonna have a hit record by the end of the summer and we ought to give him a few bookings before that happens." Eddie nodded, not really taking any notice, watching the door. Hazel continued."Tom Jones, he's the next big thing I'm telling you Ed. At least give him a chance." Eddie smiled, he could see through the window a navy blue, Ford Zephyr pulling into the parking space outside. Big Pat the wrestler and local celebrity had arrived with his wife. His attention turned back to Hazel.

"Yea, yea, just give him a couple of dates if ya like. Problem is Haze no one's ever heard of him have they, so he won't be a draw. Now there's a local band the Mods are all talking about, The Spencer Davis Group, they've got a good singer apparently, he's only sixteen but got a voice like an old black blues singer. They'll pull a big crowd and cost us fuck all."

"Ok I'll book Tom Jones, it's important we get national acts in to the club otherwise we'll be just like all the other venues in town and I'll have a look at this Mod band and see . . . " Hazel didn't finish her sentence. Eddie was out of his seat greeting his guests, patting Big Pat's shoulder as he entered the restaurant his huge frame filling the little doorway. The four sat and chatted, small talk eventually being joined by another couple of friends. The night turned into a drunken story telling contest between the men, all competing for the attention of the women and their approval. Eddie's hilarious market scams entertaining everyone and Big Pats behind the scenes tales of professional wrestling kept everyone's attention. Eddie had invited Pat to offer him a job on the door of the Cedar club. A local celebrity and hard man was just what place needed to keep the drunks under control. Pat talked things through and a deal was struck but as the two men shook hands a call from Dixie came through to Gigi's. Eddie took the call in the tiny office. Hazel kept talking to her friends but had one eye on Eddie at the other end of the restaurant. The jovial atmosphere changed when Eddie returned to the table. Hazel knew it was bad.

Eddie's face had lost its colour.

"I got a situation down town I'll be back in an hour or two. If I'm not back get a taxi, I'll see you at home, oh and do me a favour Haze, call the club tell someone to let me in round the back." Hazel knew not to ask what was happening.

"Alright Bab. Don't be late," she managed before Eddie turned and went to leave. Pat stood up as if to go with Eddie, Eddie thanked him but said he was too easily recognised for what was about to go down. He told Pat to wait with the women and left.

By the time Eddie had reached the club most of the Mods had headed home. The DJ was spinning the last few tunes of the night and people were either dancing slowly in couples or drifting off back to their particular part of the city to sleep off the drink and be ready for work in the morning. Eddie made his way through the dark streets around the back of the club. He climbed over a few walls and dropped into the rear parking spaces behind the Cedar Club. He wrapped his knuckles on the rear fire escape door. Chrissy who was waiting as arranged, opened it and the two men walked towards the front office without talking. Dixie was there, as were Don, Frankie and a couple of door staff, all stood in the dark whispering amongst themselves. Dixie was peering through little gaps of clear glass in the frosted window. He signalled Eddie to come and see. He pointed out the gunmetal Jag across the road, four men waiting inside.

"It's them," Dixie whispered.

"Who?" Eddie asked, confused.

"The Krays . . . or at least some of their gang, whoever they are, they mean business. They did Jackie Diamond over, he's in hospital." Dixie drew his finger across his throat and waited for Eddie's reply.

"Why's everyone whispering? They can't fucking hear us from here you know."

Everyone burst into laughter. "What do you mean they did Jackie over, is he dead?"

Dixie told Eddie about Jackie Diamond's injuries and how Jackie had warned Dixie. "Come away from the window and turn the fucking lights on when I give the signal." Eddie said exasperated. Dixie panicked.

"But they'll see us."

"I know, I want them to see us. Or at least see *Don*." Eddie gestured for Don to come over to the window. "Now when I say so, turn on the lights. Don, you just pace up and down the room by the window so they can see you." Don didn't move.

"If you think I'm gonna march up and down that fucking window like a duck shoot, you can go and fuck yourself!" Eddie lost his temper.

"Well either you can walk up and down that fucking window or you can come outside and actually face these bastards. They're here to kill me not you. But you are the only one of us that actually looks a bit like me so do what I'm asking you to do and stop being a twat." Don was shocked by the outburst.

"Well at least say *please*. I mean I'm risking my life here. You should've asked me nicely." Eddie looked around the room at the others.

"You see what I have to put up with for fuck's sake?" He drew a deep breath.

"OK *please* Donald, *pretty please* with fucking bells on, walk up and down by the fucking window." Don did as he was told now whilst the other men shrank away from the window. Chrissy flicked on the light switch. Don walked across the room and began pacing up and down by the window. He looked at Eddie for approval, "Is this ok?

"Don, it's not fucking Shakespeare is it? Just walk up and down the fucking room." Eddie rolled his eyes. The others began sniggering like school boys up to some secret prank, and one by one they left the room.

The Lambrianous saw the light come on and watched as the black shadow walked up and down. The tall blonde quiff easily visible from where they sat. All four sat up.

"Alright lads, show time." Chris Lambrianous patted his brother's arm."How we gonna play this then bruv?" Anthony smiled. "I'll just walk in and pop him. Anyone gets in the way you can deal with them, by the time they understand what's happening we'll be long gone."

Chris tapped Shellby's man on the shoulder. "Start the car when you see us go in and when we come out, pull up alongside the club so we can get in and then put your foot down until you get to the end of the road. Nice and slow then until we reach the hotel. I'll change the plates back and then were off back to London."

"Very smooth Mr Lambrianou." Shellby's man offered.

"Let's not start tugging each other off just yet, we gotta do the hard bit first." Chris answered.

"Nah Bruv," Anthony patted his gun, a cold smile frozen across his face, "this is gonna be fun." Chris smiled

"We all know your idea of fun is facked up Tony."

Chris put his hand on the door handle of the Jag pulling it to release the door. He stepped one foot out on to the tarmac. As he pushed his head through the car doorway beginning to stand up, he saw the image of a man running across the road from the dark side street that ran along the side of the club. By the time he realised what was happening it was too late to pull his head back into the safety of the car. The sprinting man leapt into the air and brought both feet down hard against the car door, driving it shut with such force and speed that Chris Lambrianou's head smashed through the glass of the rear window. The glass shattered around him leaving his bloody head sticking ridiculous and unconscious out of the glass hole.

The men in the front of the car reacted too slowly. If the ignition key had been turned at that point they could have gotten away but inexperience and shock clouded their reactions. Anthony knew exactly what was happening and brought up his pistol looking for a target. Outside the car Eddie had sprinted across the road carrying one of the heavy fire axes that were to be found on the walls next to the club's fire exits. Holding the axe above his head he brought it down on to the Jaguar's roof, slamming it as hard as he could into the grey metal. The axe split the roof like a tin opener, the momentum of the red axe forcing its way into the car only stopping as it came into contact with Anthony Lambrianou's scalp. The blade split the skin in the middle of his head like a surgeon's knife but luckily for all involved went no further. By shear chance Anthony had escaped death, few millimetres more and the axe would have crashed into his skull causing massive trauma and probably have killed him outright. Anthony dropped the pistol.

He held his hands to his head trying to work out why his face felt different, suddenly wet. His fingers found the bleeding gash and he tried to force the wound back together. Instead of passing out Anthony's senses became crystal clear. He saw his brother quivering with nerve endings dancing throughout his body as he hung unconsciously from the rear window. SMASH! The axe came through the roof again and again. He ducked low on to the back seat. His hands searching the dark red carpet on the car floor for the gun. The back window exploded, showering him in glass. He heard men shouting outside and the doors of the car being opened. Two hands grabbed at his ankles and dragged him across the leather seat. He grabbed feebly at the red leather but he had no strength left in him to keep them at bay.

Eddie stood on top of the domed Jaguar's roof smashing the axe into the metal. He couldn't stop himself from laughing uncontrollably, he looked down as Chrissy and Frankie dragged the two men in the front seat out, clubbing them mercilessly around their heads with two foot long lead pipes. The two doormen were wrestling with the man in the back seat, one on each leg pulling as hard as they could. Dixie hung back not wanting to be too involved but couldn't help himself from running into the affray every now and then delivering a kick or two to the helpless assassins. Chrissy on the other hand had lost himself in the beating, pummelling the driver senseless with the soft lead pipe. Frankie had dropped his pipe and was busy stomping his heels into the man, as his victim tried to protect himself with his arms wrapped around his head. Eddie jumped off the car and joined the doormen dragging Anthony Lambrianous from the back seat. Anthony found the cold metal of the gun under the passengers seat, he fumbled the gun into the right position in his hand and let himself be dragged from the car. As his head and torso fell from the leather seat on to the road he flipped himself around and fired a shot at the figure in front of him. His aim was good but his luck was out, the shot hit Eddie square in the chest nearly knocking him over. Eddie kicked the pistol from his hands and brought his heel down hard on his the Cockney's already blood- soaked face, breaking his nose and knocking him unconscious. The beatings stopped and all eyes were on Eddie. He stood up waving off Dixie's help.

"I'm fine I'm fine," he said angrily.

The brothers looked at each other, stunned that Eddie could have withstood a point blank direct hit. Dixie grabbed Eddie's sheepskin coat and yanked it open expecting to see a red blood stained rag but instead found black powder burns where the cartridge had misfired. "You lucky bastard!" Dixie began laughing. "Fucking hell Ed you are one lucky fucker." he continued. Chrissy and Frankie gathered around both opening the coat to see the burned cotton shirt underneath.

"Yea but look at me shirt! Fucking ruined now, brand new that was. I'm gonna charge that to the club, cheeky bastards." Ed said bravely, hiding his now shaking hands as the adrenalin of shock began to kick in.

"If he'd have got off one more round you'd be a dead man Ed." said Dixie patting Eddie on the shoulders. "What now then lads?" He turned to the group. "What do we do with them now? What about him?" Dixie pointed at the man that had been sitting in the front passenger's seat but was now beaten and bloody, gibbering under his breath on the black tarmac. Chrissy spoke.

"This one's not a cockney he's a Brummie," he said, poking the driver's head with the lead pipe, he knelt down beside the man and began riffling his pockets. The man made no protest. "There's nothing here except personal shit. So who are you?" The man sat, hands above his head, staring around at the men towering over him. Chrissy gave him a slap around the face. The man came to his senses.

"I work for Tom Shellby. I'm just a bookie, he asked me to drive these two around. I ain't no killer I'm just a bookie." Chrissy patted the man on the head and chuckled

"Oh you're a bookie are ya? Well I must remember to tell that to poor Jackie Diamond, you nearly cut his fucking head off . . . Just a bookie, well I'll bet you hundred to one, you ain't too happy about this. You didn't kill him did ya? Jackie's still alive." The man burst into tears,

"I've got a wife and kids. I'm just a driver." Chrissy slapped the man again.

"Shut it bookie, you're gonna get what's coming mate!" he went to slap him again but Eddie grabbed his hand.

"We can sort this out later." Eddie began to take charge, coming back to his senses. "Get em back in the car and bring it round the back of the club. I can see blue flashing lights in the distance so let's get them out of sight sharpish and let Dixie deal with his own." Eddie stopped suddenly, his scowl turning into a broad grin and bursting into laughter he pointed at the illuminated office above the club, "For fuck's sake, someone tell Don he can stop walking up and down now!" They moved as one, sniggering, picking the victims up by hands and feet and piling them into the rear car seat as best they could. Chrissy gathered the lead pipes and Eddie's axe and ran back inside the club. From the start of the fight to the clean up it had only been eight minutes. Eight minutes that would send a message from the Birmingham underworld to the London mobs saying STAY OUT!

The police turned up blue lights flaring and bells ringing. Someone had reported the beatings from behind one of the twitching net curtains from the flats above the shops that lined the road. Dixie flashed his badge and told the two uniformed officers to turn off their sirens and fuck off. They did as they were told, without question. Dixie had a reputation now and was respected amongst the lower ranks.

As the dark blue police car drove into the night Dixie stood in the middle of the road, watching the cars red lights get smaller and smaller until they vanished. After the fight and the police sirens, the silence was deafening. He stood drinking in the peaceful silence knowing it wouldn't last long. Slowly the low hum of the city began to creep into the air and Dixie knew the next few hours wouldn't be pleasant ones. He turned and strolled back into the club. Don was waiting by the door.

"How did I do? Was it alright?" Dixie laughed.

"You were fucking brilliant Don, a real Hamlet" The joke was lost on Don. To Don *Hamlet* were a make of cigars. Dixie became serious. "What happens now?" The policeman was expecting some kind of gangster reply.

"I don't fucking know what *just* happened never mind what's about to happen. Eddie will sort it!"

Eddie had retreated into the club. He called Hazel and he could hear the relief in her voice. He told her what had happened but didn't mention the gunshot and how he had to make arrangements for the Cockneys to be returned to London and what to do with Shellby's men. She seemed unfazed by the details.

"The Irish club, Small Heath." Eddie went silent and let Hazel's crackly voice continue. "The Irish club just started work on a club car park." Hazel let the words sink in, a few seconds past by in silence, "I'm just saying if you want to dump some rubbish then that's the place to do it." Eddie couldn't see it, but Hazel was rolling her eyes on the other end of the phone. Eddie still stayed silent. "Eddie? Eddie are you there?" Hazel thought the line had gone dead.

"Yea, Yea, I heard ya Bab, but it's not like that." His mind was wandering back to the gunshot. A cold sweat rose on his forehead and he felt a tremble in his heart. Hazel's voice had brought him back to the real world. The adrenaline had worn off now and shock began to kick in. "No we're gonna return the goods Bab, I'll call you back when we've finished." he snapped into the phone.

"Are you ok?" Hazel's voice sounded concerned but Eddie just placed the receiver on its hook.

Eddie walked back into the main dance hall. The brothers, Dixie and the doormen were drinking shots and talking in low tones amongst themselves. Eddie strode into the middle and clapped his hands together.

"Right let's get these cunts back to London. Chrissy give Tom the truck a bell tell him we've got a job for him." Chrissy looked at his watch.

"Ed it's two o'clock in the fucking morning."

"I don't give a fuck what time it is. This has got to happen *now.* I want those pair of Cockney wankers to wake up and find that car in the middle of the Kray's East End or wherever it is those fuckers come from. We've got to send a message: If they come to Birmingham they get fucked!" Chrissy rose and headed to the office without a word. Eddie turned to the others.

"You two get them Londoners, tie em up and leave em in the car park," he pointed at Don and Frankie, "Don, Frankie stay with them!" He turned to the doormen. "Get rid of Shellby's men, give em a good hiding, send em on their way. I don't want to see or hear of them again. Understand?"

The doormen nodded and left happy to have a job to do. Don and Frankie finished their drinks and left. Dixie and Eddie were left alone. Dixie could see Eddie was shaken but firm. He went behind the bar and poured two whiskys. Eddie sat down on a bar stool and the two men faced each other.

"There's always some cunt that wants you dead." Eddie sipped the whisky.

"Yea there always will be too, Ed." Dixie raised his glass and chinked it with Eddie's.

"We were lucky tonight Dixie. If Jackie Diamond hadn't tipped us off, one of us would be dead right now. "Dixie nodded agreement.

"It ain't over yet Ed. They're gonna come back bigger and harder.

Even if they give up on Brum you've rubbed their nose in shit and the Krays can't be seen to have that happen to them. If you rattle the cage don't be surprised if the monkey comes out fighting."

Eddie laughed. He knew Dixie thought it was a bad idea sending the Lambrianous back to London even if he didn't say so. But Eddie had learnt the hard way that hard men react to *strength* not weakness. If the Fewtrells showed weakness it was over and the Krays would move in and take over.

"Ha, fuck the monkey! Did you see what I did to that bear?" Both men laughed. Frankie stepped back into the room and without saying anything joined the two, pouring himself a drink.

"What's so funny?"

"Eddie's gonna shoot a monkey," Dixie explained and he and Eddie burst into laughter. Frankie looked confused.

"Maybe I'll choke a chicken" Eddie continued, Dixie sniggered, "More like stuff a turkey!"

"You leave Hazel out of it mate." Ed answered, both men laughing. Frankie's face was frozen in a small scowl.

"You two are fucking mental. What the fuck are you on about?" Chrissy had returned from the office and viewing the scene he looked at Frankie for an explanation as to what was so funny.

Frankie just shrugged his broad shoulders and carried on drinking.

"Tom the truck's on his way." Chrissy said over the laughter not sure if Eddie had heard him or not. "He'll be here in ten minutes." The laughter continued, becoming almost hysterical. The two were letting off the steam, built up from the events outside. Only Eddie and Dixie really understood the seriousness of what had just happened. Things could've been so different tonight if they hadn't been tipped off by Jackie Diamond and the gunshot Anthony Lambrianous had aimed point blank at Eddie hadn't been a faulty shell causing the misfire. Their relief just showed itself in boyish banter. What else were they going to do? Men like this don't shed tears of relief.

Tom the truck had turned up moaning about the hour. Eddie met him and handed over one hundred pounds, a month's money for the fat little man. His little oil stained stubby fingered hands grabbed the cash and stuffed it in his pocket without asking about what the job involved. Eddie explained that the car was a right off and he wanted it crushed and dropped off outside the Blind Beggar pub Whitechapel Road, London . . . *before sunrise.* Eddie saw a certain look in Tom's eyes and continued fixing the little man's darting eyes.

"Understand what I'm saying to you. Don't fuck about thinking your gonna keep the car Tom. I want it to be crushed and delivered. If it ain't there by sunrise I'll come and take my cash back *with interest.*

Understand?"

Tom the truck nodded and was gone. His little legs scampering across the rear car park to his truck cab, he climbed up the step like some kind of strange little animal and into his cab. The scruffy old pick up truck burst into smoky life. Tom switched on a light at the back of the wagon and the whole car park was illuminated. The pick up bed began to tilt and Tom jumped from the wagon, dragging a chain across the cobbles he hooked the chain under the front of the Jaguar then sprang back in his cab. The chain dragged back into the winch until it became taught and the Jag began to move onto the back of the wagon. When the car came to rest on top of the flat bed Tom tilted it back and turned off the engine. The Fewtrell Brothers watched on amazed at the little man's strength and the speed of his operation. Tom climbed onto the flat bed and began tying down the car. Tom the truck may have been plenty of things but he wasn't stupid, never once looking inside in case he saw something he shouldn't. He finished the job and was gone.

Anthony Lambrianous sat bound at Don's feet, his still unconscious brother Chris lying on the cold wet compounded mud car park floor beside him. Anthony struggling, bleeding in the corner of the car park watching his bosses car being taken away to the crusher on to the little blue Bedford truck, rage pulsing through the veins in his forehead and the words of Ronnie Kray ringing in his head. "*Don't fuck it up.*"

The Cube on the Cross Road

Chapter 18

In the early nineteen sixties Monday mornings around the Whitechapel Road were always a busy ones. The air hung heavy with exhaust fumes and the rumble of red busses. Barrow boys pushed their trundling wooden, steel rapped wheeled trollies to market or street corners, rattling along the old paving stones and cobbles, bringing Victorian London crashing into the modern age with a cacophony of noise, flat caps and fag smoke; the only protection the market boys needed against the soft, grey drizzle that gave this place a sense of old world mystery at any given time of the year.

A traffic jam had wound it's way up the Whitechapel Road. Horns beeped and people stood beside their cars cursing the delay. Scooters and motorbikes drove along the pavements to escape the standstill. A group of men stood around a gun metal grey cube that sat in the middle of the T-junction that connected the Whitechapel Road with Maple Street just outside the Blind Beggar public house. Like a scene from a science fiction movie the men stood at a distance watching the cube as if at some point it would burst into life and kill them all. The police were called but when they arrived even they were also non plussed and just stood at a distance. The alien grey cube wasn't the cause of fear amongst the watching, growing crowd, it was the black and white car number plate left standing on its end on top of the cube, *XSV 902*, Ronnie Kray's number plate. Everyone around the East End knew it and everyone knew, even the police, that they couldn't get involved. This was gang stuff: an insult, a threat, a warning from another gang who knew. The one thing that was for sure, there would be blood spilt over this and almost on cue, the drizzle soaked traces of dark red paint on the cube began to liquify and run into the black tarmac and it became apparent to all the bystanders that somewhere in the small mass of twisted gunmetal grey there were human remains.

The night before the cube appeared in the East End, Eddie's two doormen stood in the muddy car park at the back of the Cedar Club Birmingham looking at the two beaten Brummies that worked for Tom Shellby.

"Well Eddie said get rid of em." The burly balding doorman confirmed Eddie Fewtrell's command to the other man.

"Please lads I'm just a bookie," Shellby's man pleaded, but was rewarded with a kick in the kidneys. The other doorman pointed at the Jag.

"If he's gonna get rid of that car then I'm gonna have it." he said stroking his hand across the shiny paint of the domed roof.

"Ha, what about Eddie's axe holes in the roof and the windows it's gonna cost you a fucking fortune to fix this up. Anyway, why should you have it to yourself? Let's just take it and sell it scrap, it's still worth a few quid. Eddie said he wanted it towed away so let's just stick these two cunts in the boot and take it, we can dump them in the countryside get back into town sell it to a scrap yard and split the cash. Eddie will never know fuck all. He'll just assume the tow truck took it and we did what he asked."

The two men just shook hands without saying a word and the beating began with a new energy and cruelty. By the time Shellby's men were piled into the trunk of the Jag neither of them either knew or cared were they were. They lay there in the dark hoping, bleeding, sobbing. Before the boot lid closed, one of the doormen pulled a small black bag from the car then slammed the lid trapping the men inside. Outside they could hear the doormen talking about the bag, but couldn't work out what was happening, then the sound of two, very happy men as they discovered the £2000 hidden within the small black holdall. They talked about what they should do, to tell Eddie or not. Shellby's man started to kick the boot sending both men into a panic. As he lay in the tiny space with his unconscious associate the argument was about car keys, one blaming the other for losing them. Neither thought to look in the ignition of the car where they had been all along. By the time they had, Tom the truck had shown up and the doormen had missed their chance of a bit of quick cash from the sale of the Jaguar. The little bag was thrown into the corner of the dark car park to which they both withdrew into the shadows and stayed silent and just watched as the scene played out before them.

Don and Frankie dragged the two Cockneys out of the rear corridor of the club into the car park and dumped them on the ground. Then Eddie and the Dixie stepped out into the dark space and the little man in the blue Bedford turned on the flood lights, illuminating the stage as the players acted out their roles before the doormen's eyes. Eddie handed the little man some cash and it dawned on them what was happening. The balding doorman went to step forward and tell Eddie about the men in the car boot, but he was dragged back into the shadows by the other man who pleaded.

"Don't be fucking stupid. If you tell the Fewtrells about them blokes in the boot they'll work out what we were planning and it'll be *us* in the fucking boot!"

They pressed their backs against the old brick wall that surrounded the car park and stayed hidden in the shadows hoping not to be noticed. The two men watched the car being loaded and disappear into the night in a cloud of diesel smoke. They had unwittingly sent two men to a horrible death through their greedy actions. A moment or two of regret shared between them soon disappeared. Shellby's men were gone and wouldn't be coming back. As far as they were concerned they'd had a close shave but in the end a job well done. As Tom the truck drove off they reappeared from the shadows, hands in pockets and slim smiles on their faces and joined everyone else as they discussed what they would do with the Lambrianous brothers, the little black bag still hidden in the shadows. Only one of the doorman ever worked for the Fewtrells again. After pretending to save up £2000 from his wages he went on to open a very successful, used car lot on the Coventry Road, the other found *another* sort of opening beneath a car park in front of an Irish club in Small Heath and is probably still there to this day.

The Kray brothers had to walk most of the way down the Mile End Road. The traffic was a joke. They had been told about the cube by one of their crew who had been waiting for the Blind Beggar pub to open but wanted to see it for themselves. They had given permission to the police to shift the crushed car from the T-junction, but the traffic Jam continued as drivers rubbernecked to see what the fuss was all about. Ron and Reg stood looking at the cube scowling.

The brothers assumed it was what was left of the Lambrianous inside, but a phone call from Anthony Lambrianous later that morning explaining the circumstances of the crushed car and it's contents made a bad situation worse. But the Krays were happy to hear their old pals were still alive. Recriminations for their failure would come later. For the moment they had to deal with the embarrassment of this insult in front of the whole of the East End. To make matters worse their arch enemies the Richardson brothers had taken advantage of the moment and sent a funeral wreath over to the Blind Beggar saying *Sorry for your loss.* The joke was lost on both Ron and Reg.

"Bastards. I'll facking skin em alive those stupid Iti cunts." Ronnie was ranting as he stormed up and down the bar of the Blind Beggar. Reg sat drinking a gin and tonic far more cooler than his brother. The pub was shut so luckily there were no witnesses to the rant. Ronnie was right though, something had to give.

"We need to get these Birmingham cunts once and for all or the next thing you know they'll be moving in on *us.*" Ronnie stopped pacing and started out the window at the crowd gathering around the crushed car. The sight made him flare up again.

"We're gonna be the laughing stock of London now for fack's sake.

!" He rapped his knuckles on the window. "FACK OFF!" The sight of Ronnie Kray was enough to send the sightseers scampering off like surprised cockroaches.

Reg huffed, silently bored of his brother's tantrums, sipping the gin he shook his head deciding cruelly to wind up his highly strung twin. "Nice wreath though," he said smirking. Ronnie exploded

"Nice Wreath! . . . *Nice facking wreath!* Is that all you can say? We look a right pair of cunts now don't we? We've got to have revenge on the Richardsons and the Fewtrells *now!* I want them facking dead, all of em. "

"That's your answer to everything ain't it. Facking kill em, shoot em, murder, death, power. You need to pull your head out your arse and start thinking things through!" Ron was shocked. Reg had never talked to him like this before.

"Who do you think you're facking talking to? I ain't one of your little tarts. You talk to me like that I'll facking knock you out." Reg laughed and stood up.

"Well here you go Ron," he pointed at his chin, "give it a go and see what happens!"

The two brothers squared up. They hadn't fought for years. They had put up a united front when the other members of the Firm were around, even when they totally disagreed with each other, at which point their mother had always stepped in. But their egos had gotten bigger as they had spread their wings and with their success they had become totally unapproachable.

The fight started with a few pushes, argy bargy mainly, but punches were thrown as the brothers became more vexed and the fight became vicious. Things had begun to spin out of control around the Kray brothers and maybe this was just a way of dealing with the pressure of success. After fifteen minutes of brawling the steam had all but dissipated. The bar was wreaked and the twins sat in a mess of broken stools, tipped tables and broken bottles and glasses. Bloody and exhausted they looked at each other in silence. Ashamed, Reggie spoke first.

"If our mum could see us now she'd facking kill us Ron." He laughed.

Ron picked himself up and dusted his black suit down, reaching down he held his hand out to his brother. Reg grabbed it and pulled himself off the sticky pub carpet. As he stood up Ronnie grabbed him and pulled him in tight into his shoulder.

"Sorry bruv." he said almost in tears. He rested his head on his brothers shoulder. Reg drew him in. They held each other for a while before the noise of the city outside broke up the bonding. Ron sat in one of the old bar chairs and plonked his feet on the table. Reg went back behind the bar and poured two whiskys. He came and sat opposite his twin.

"There you go bruv. You see fighting ain't gonna get us anywhere is it? That crushed car is still out there on the Old Mile Road with everyone stood around staring at it. Those Italian twats we sent to do the job let us down, those Brummie bastards seem to be one step ahead of us every time and we are still the laughing stock of the East End. But if we fight each other we'll lose the lot Ron. The Richardsons or someone else will move in as soon as they see us fall apart." Ron nodded.

"Yea, yea I'm sorry Reg but we *need* a plan. Those Fewtrells are making us look like a pair of facking monkeys. If we can beat em once and for all, things will slip back into place, I know it! We'll be setting an example."

"We need an old fashioned solution to this," Reg had perked up now, a plan forming, "until now we've tried to be clever bastards. Get the job done without getting our hands dirty. You can't trust anyone with this cos they're all facking idiots Ron. We got to sort it ourselves. We need to sort this the way they did in the *old* days." The brothers looked at each other in silence. Reggie shifted in his seat, brows furrowed, he leant forward.

"You mean as in the *old* old days? Big gang fights, proper fights man on man?" Reg smiled.

"Yea you've got it bruv, remember Dad used to tell us about the big fights down the dock yards in the old days, five or six hundred men in a pitch battle. He said they always sorted out the problems between the unions and the old mob. In the end the last man standing held the ground.“ Ron stood and started to pace up and down the bar like a modern day Napoleon, hands behind his back looking deep in thought. This was the type of thing he was born to do, it was his destiny to lead men or so his ego believed. He had rehearsed the pace many times in front of the Firm members and had always given the impression to them that he was in control, but like many things about Ronnie Kray it was just a front to hide behind. At this moment in time, this was just the type of attitude the twins needed.

“I think you might be right Reggie, we'll turn up en masse and just take over. What are they gonna do?” Reg tried to keep level headed. “Hold on we need to plan this properly. Dad used to say that both sides need to agree to it, then there's always an over all winner. It has to be an agreement.” “And if they refuse?”

“We tell em we're coming anyway. If they roll over then all's the better.” Ron became animated. “How many men can we get together? I mean real hard bastards, shooters or hand to hand? Yea I can see it now, me and you like generals overseeing the whole thing, leading them into battle.” Ron held his head high, staring out of the window in a teutonic daydream. Reggie sighed.

“Get a grip Ron, this is gonna take a lot of organising. We need to keep it quiet until it's time to strike, but at the same time we need to get people onboard. Swear em to secrecy.” The more Reggie spoke, the more Ron got carried away with his medieval fantasy. Reg had to bring him back to reality by giving him a job to do. “Make a list Ron.”

“A list?”

“Yeah, a list of the people we're gonna take with us to Birmingham, people we can trust. Stick the Lambrianous at the top, they owes us one for facking up the hit in the first place.” Ron walked behind the bar and began to search for a pen and paper.

“Where are they anyway?”

“Dunno, the call was from a phone box, it was Tony apparently, Chris is in a bad way. They took a beating. That's all I know bruv.” The two brothers sat in the bar and began drawing up a list of the most infamous characters they could think of; names of enforcers, henchmen, mental cases or anyone with a reputation for violence was written down. The lads in the Firm would be included without question and anyone they felt could be an asset but didn't want to help out would be leant on until they offered assistance.

The day outside the Blind Beggar carried on as it did everyday. People coming and going about their business. The metal cube stayed there all day with groups of shoppers and commuters giving it the once over on their way to wherever it was they were heading. The police stayed away but at the end of school time around fifty kids gathered around it. One or two brave ones climbing on top to the loud cheers of the other kids. Everyone seemed to have forgotten the two passengers inside who ironically were on their first and last trip to London. As the day rolled on, members of the Firm came and gathered at the Blind Beggar and by lunch time the Kray brothers were both drunk. Knowing they were surrounded by their friends they talked freely about their plans for an *invasion* of Birmingham. Other names were offered for their list. Ron paced up and down for effect. Weapons were discussed. Everyone was anxious for the return of the Lambrianous brothers and to hear what they had to say for themselves. Ron and Reg were undecided what to do with them. They were old family friends after all, but they had royally fucked things up and created this whole problem. The Krays had a reputation to uphold now, more than ever so an example had to be made whether they liked it or not.

Waifs and Strays

Chapter 19

The summer was a hot one. Birmingham was always a dusty place, but this year the heat seemed to make it more so than ever. The newspapers and radio told of southerly warm winds blowing in red dust from the Sierra desert but if it did, no one noticed, everything was dusty in the summer in the city. Life went on as usual. No one missed the two men from Tom Shellby's bookies that disappeared except their wives and kids. They complained to the police but it went no further.

Eddie's club grew from strength to strength, along with success came celebrity which brought its own problems. Firstly, every nutter who fancied himself a gangster turned up on the club door asking for a job or to do a job. Crazy money-making schemes were constantly on his desk from ex cons to ex army. Hit men from the suburbs that had never seen a gun and turned up on the bus in second hand suits offering to "take out" his enemies. Most were just given a drink and pushed out the door but anyone that looked a bit handy was kept on for a rainy day. The second problem that fame brought was women: in many cases just as dangerous as the hit men. Suddenly all the brothers had women hanging from their arms. Of course the brothers Fewtrell told each of the girls that *they* owned the club and they had Eddie running it for them. To begin with it was just a bit of a laugh, but soon some of the women were regular girlfriends and began asking questions.

"Why does Eddie earn more money than you?"

"How come if it's your club Eddie tells you what to do?"

"Why has Hazel got a Mercedes and you're driving around in that shit heap?"

Awkward questions all and it wasn't long before pride and jelousy began to do it's work amongst the brothers, driving gaps between them and creating a set of chinks in their amour that would stay there for many years after. Eddie was oblivious to any and all of his disgruntled brothers grievances, as a matter of fact he was really in his stride and he was making noise about another club, now that the cash had really started to flow. Just to think two years ago he was selling stockings at the Rag market and now he had more money than he knew what to do with. Money had given him confidence as well as a good dose of paranoia. The Fewtrell family and a crew of relatives and friends calling themselves the Whizz Mob went through the Birmingham gang scene like a dose of salts. After finding out about Shellby's men giving information to the Krays, everyone was under suspicion. Birmingham lakes and building sites became makeshift graveyards for anyone they didn't like the look of. In an effort to clean up the city of anyone that was against them they drew a line in the sand that either brought people onside or sent them to the pig farm. Soon the Whizz Mob had grown to huge numbers of around two or three hundred friends and loose family, spread across the city, all looking out for each other with Eddie Fewtrell at its centre. Everyone was welcome, black, white, Irish, gypsy, Brummie or Police made no difference, as long as you could be trusted.

Shillelagh Law

Chapter 20

Tensions in Northern Ireland began to mount between Protestants and Catholics that summer too. The first seeds of something serious happening in Northern Ireland began to be mentioned in the British newspapers, stirring up a racist reaction against the Irish in the UK. The Birmingham IRA began to flex it's muscles around the town, collecting money on behalf of the *cause*. The *Cause* as it was referred to, still had, for many, that old time 1916 uprising romance about it. Raising money for arms and the IRA was still looked upon by many as something to connect them to the country they loved, but because of financial strife or for the want of a better life, had to leave. Many of the Birmingham Irish could remember first hand the brutality of the Black and Tans and their indiscriminate killing of family and friends only fifty years before.

The higher than normal IRA attention in the media increased antiirish prejudice from the predominantly *English* pub landlords, who then barred anyone with an Irish accent from almost every pub, club and venue in the city. Prejudice against the Irish and black populations in Birmingham was just an accepted part of life in the early sixties and to see a sign on a pub or hotel door saying no Irish, Blacks or Dogs, even in the Irish and Black areas of the city, was not an uncommon sight. After a few weeks of this media attention the Irish were forced to socialise in one of two places, either the Irish Centre in Digbeth or the Gary Owen in Small Heath. There were a few smaller catholic social clubs in the suburbs but these were usually run by committees made up of older, first generation Irish who had their feet firmly stuck in the past and lacked the modern day swinging sixties appeal that the Cedar club had. Eddie saw the gap in the market and welcomed the Irish in as if he were one of them. The Fewtrells didn't ask questions, they just took money: whatever race, colour, religion or sexuality, they all had cash and to Eddie that made them all equal. Many of the hardcore Birmingham Irish were now part of the Whizz Mob and whether Eddie knew it of not he had a small Irish army at his fingertips. Little did he know that by the end of the year he would need one.

London swung harder than ever, The Beatles were being chased up the charts by the rest of the copy cat beat groups and the first seeds of Psychedelia could be spotted on Carnaby Street. Beautiful young hipsters could be seen driving around the capital in tiny Mini-Moke jeeps or E-types, showing they were way ahead of the in-crowd. Three button, small lapel suits had given way to paisley shirts and cravats with the odd post box red royal guard's tunic thrown on top, giving a hint at *Sergeant Pepper* about to arrive at some time in the near future.

The Krays were feeling the pinch, it was great having the celebrities at your club but it wasn't so great when they brought the media with them often followed by the police and tax man dragging up the rear. Things were closing in and both brothers could unconsciously feel things coming to a head, possibly even see the end, Ronnie more than Reg.

Reggie was fulfilled with his new wife, controlling yet besotted with her, much to Ronnie's disgust. Ronnie withdrew in to the homosexual underworld of London, where perverse bizarre parties brought him some release from the pressure of being a celebrity gangster. Speed and LSD were the order of the day, neither of which suited Ronnie's personality sending him into every increasing mood swings and tantrums. He never thought to try the heroin, he was so happily testing on others, which may have helped him stay straighter in his mind. Every time he was high, the Birmingham thorn in his side pricked him a little bit harder until he ended up just ranting about his army taking over the city and how he would walk the corridors of power. He was losing his grip on reality and the other gang lords and hard men of London could smell their downfall. All they had to do was wait.

Word had gone around that the Krays needed bodies, lots of bodies for a trip up north. No details, just that you needed to be able to handle yourself and it helped if you had experience with weapons and if you were in need of a bit of cash they would sort that out too. They couldn't let any of the other local gangs know about their plans, so word had been spread in the far flung regions, away from the East End, such as Camden and Kentish town in North London only five or six miles from Whitechapel, but a world apart in the sixties. The only problem for the Krays was that Camden and Kentish town were both strong London Irish communities, packed with Irish families that had been there for generations many of whom had family connections in Birmingham. So when the word came through about the *call to arms, p*hone calls to Birmingham were made and questions were asked and the secret was leaked. Of course the Krays had no way of keeping this thing quiet for long, that was just another of Ronnie's fantasies.

Inevitably, towards the end of the summer Eddie Fewtrell was approached by the leading members of the Birmingham IRA and given the heads up about the Cockney army about to come north to take over the city. Even in an era of no CCTV and unsophisticated Police surveillance, the plan was ambitious. Four or five hundred of London's hardest, meanest enforcers getting on a train to battle over England's second city seemed a ridiculous idea but in the twisted minds of the Krays and their sycophants there was no other solution, and with no one willing or brave enough to say no, the plan went ahead regardless.

The call to Birmingham was made personally by Ronnie. A date was set and terms were agreed. Eddie wasn't around the Cedar club to talk to Ronnie Kray but Don, almost as good a master at the dramatic as Ronnie, took the call and between the two of them they warbled on for nearly an hour, firstly with threats and counter threats, then a more formal conversation gave way to banter and even laughter. By the time the two men put their phones down they had both forgotten the reason why they had talked in the first place. Ronnie wondered why Don wasn't running the Birmingham mob instead of Eddie as he seemed far more approachable. Don on the other hand spent the rest of the day telling anyone that would listen that he had just spent the morning talking to the famous Ronnie Kray, very proud of himself. He told Eddie of the conversation, remarking about how Ronnie Kray seemed like a decent bloke. Eddie exploded.

"Those Cockney cunts tried to kill me you fucking idiot," He pulled his sheepskin coat off the hook behind the door and threw it at Don. "There, take a look at the bullet hole. You think he's your mate . . . well he ain't. They tried to get me and they won't think twice about killing you either. They ain't coming up here for tea and cake you know, they're coming here to take over, which means we . . . yea you and me might end up at the bottom of the fucking grand canal. You need to stop pouncing around Don cause this might all go pear shaped faster than you can say knife. Now fuck off and do what you're paid to do, whatever that is these days!" Don left, tail between his legs and never mentioned the phone call again.

The Lambrianous Brothers were back on the scene. Chris's head injury had left him hospitalised for weeks and Anthony had been laying low for quite some time, they chose to make their appearance at a good moment when the Kray twins were in good spirits. Mrs Kray had given her sons a sharp dressing down about any kind of talk about payback on the Lambrianous.

"They're old family friends, the East End won't take it well if we turn on our own." She drove home the point by holding her wooden spoon in hand as if to hit the boys with it as she had when they were little kids. Following their mothers advice the brothers greeted Chris and Anthony with pats on the back and jokes about the crushed car. The Lambrianous were relieved and to add conviction to their loyalty to the Firm they talked non stop about revenge on the Fewtrells, only too happy when told of the plans to invade Birmingham, gang handed. Secretly, both had doubts about the idea, having seen first hand what the Fewtrells were capable of. Nevertheless the list of names grew longer and weapons began to be stock piled as the day for the battle grew nearer.

Two sides to a Fence.

Chapter 21

Dixie had been busy with trivial matters all summer. He had been asked by his superiors to form what was to become known as the Serious Crime Squad for the West Midlands. Their task was to infiltrate crime gangs and families or terrorist groups and bring them down in whatever way possible. He had been secretly dreaming and working on this since he had met Eddie that first time outside the Bermuda club. Now he was recruiting within the force for new maverick officers that were willing to work outside normal police practice and go deep undercover for long periods of time. He was under pressure from the top to repay Eddie for his help up the Police ladder by setting him up for a fall. His superiors were only too happy with his apparent progress and were willing to enable him in anyway they could. Dixie wasn't happy about their ambitions and felt caught between a rock and a hard place, his loyalty tested to the maximum.

There was only one problem with West Midland's Police plans, Eddie Fewtrell had also been recruiting in the police force. Young officers were easily brought on side with bribes of sex, money or information about criminal activity that would help their career and their superiors' plans soon leaked out. Eddie was gutted to hear about Dixie's plans for Eddie's downfall but didn't show it. Most of the time he was so manic it was hard to tell *what* he was thinking, so nothing seemed array to Dixie. Eddie was not convinced the rumours were true, Dixie had put his neck on the line plenty of times for the Fewtrell's. Eddie was increasingly paranoid these days though so at some point he knew he would have to confront Dixie about which side of the fence he was sitting on. Eddie knew if it was the wrong side, Dixie would have to pay the price with a pound of flesh.

Eddie called Dixie in to the club office and told him about the phone call and the gang fight proposed by the Krays. He asked him for his opinion about when and where. Dixie was shocked Eddie had agreed to it but in the back of his mind he knew it would be a good chance for the police to sweep in after the fight and nick everyone in one fell swoop, thus cleaning both Birmingham *and* London of some of it's most infamous criminals. If it worked he would be a hero. Eddie pressed him to have Snow Hill railway station cleared of the public so they could settle things once and for all. Dixie agreed to talk to his superiors but promised nothing, instead changing the subject to Jackie Diamond.

"Have you seen him recently?" Dixie left the question hanging.

"Nah, he's gone to ground, after filling you in about who attacked him he's probably been in hiding since the run in with the Lambrianous brothers." Eddie guessed.

"So he's still alive then. I mean you haven't done anything *silly* have you? Remember he was the one that saved your life." Dixie questioned.

"What kind of a question is that? Don't tell me you're finally turning into a real copper after all this time, *Inspector?*" Eddie spat, "you need to remember that if it weren't for me you'd still be trying to ride that fucking horse on the beat. You need to decide which side you're on pal."

Dixie was genuinely shocked.

"And you need to stop being so paranoid *Mr Fewtrell.* Have I ever let you down? Have I? . . . I thought we had a you scratch my back I'll scratch yours situation here."

"Yea well that depends on how many backs you're scratching don't it? You'd better trot on Dixie, your bosses might be missing you." Eddie said staring at him unflinching. Dixie stood up and turned to the door.

"I'll be in touch about Snow Hill station." He slammed the office door without looking back leaving Eddie sitting with his dark thoughts behind the dark oak desk. He'd never argued with Dixie before, it didn't feel good but he couldn't help but give in to his paranoia about the man. Time would tell if his suspicions were true. In London, Ronnie insisted the show down was to take place on the 14th of October. The anniversary of the Battle of Hastings 1066. It was all he talked about, how William the Conquerer had defeated Harold and won the kingship of England. The other members of the Firm mocked him behind his back in subdued tones, but all of them hoped his enthusiasm would bring them a victory over the Whizz Mob. Reg, on the other hand was more interested in the smaller but more important details, like how they would get there, where they would stay once they won the fight, who they would leave behind to run things and of course what weapons they should bring. Ronnie insisted they wouldn't use guns unless things got out of hand. He wanted to keep this,

"An honourable fight."

He had images of medieval battles running through his mind and saw himself, sword in hand leading the charge. The inner crew of the Firm had started calling him King Ron much to Reggie's amusement.

As the day drew nearer the Firm began to introduce outsiders into the inner circle at the Blind Beggar and Ronnie took great delight in welcoming them like some kind of ancient warlord, making them swear their fealty to him and Reg. The whole affair had a fantasy feel about it, apart from all the weapons usually at the Firms disposal, people began to arrive at the pub and open up old canvas bags or wraps with ancient, antique swords and knives in them, presenting them to one of the brothers as if to win favour with their new masters. Guns, there were lots of guns: shotguns, sawn offs, hunting rifles, old World War Two carbines that had seen better days, there were pistols, revolvers, a colt 45 and even a beautiful pair of duelling pistols in perfect working order, stolen from one of the many stately homes on the outskirts of London. All were laid on the tables of the Blind Beggar. Ronnie took a liking to the duelling flintlocks straight away, the young fence who had brought them in was paid off immediately and the boxed antique flintlocks were taken back to have pride of place at the Kray family home. In later years as their problems mounted, Ron would take great delight in holding the old pistols, spending hours gazing at the weapons, lost in thought.

One hundred and twenty miles north up the M1 and M6 motorways things were far less professional. All the Whizz Mob could muster were billy clubs, pick axe handles and the odd cricket bat. There was talk of guns but few actually materialised. These weren't real gangsters or villains, these were scrappers, boozers, wannabes and football hooligans out for a fight. Few of them had ever heard of the Krays and even if they had, they were more than confident with the city hard-knocks that had shown up to the meeting at the Cedar Club. In fact so many had turned up they had to adjourn to the car park behind the club. Eddie and his brothers stood at the centre of the group which numbered between six and seven hundred. Eddie wasn't into speeches so Don took the soap box. He was looking his best in a dark blue velvet, double breasted, six button suit and cravat, his lacquered quiff waving slightly in the evening breeze, looking more like a young prince than a club operator, in complete contrast to the down on their luck working class scruffy crew facing him dressed in donkey jackets, parkas and cheap Burton off the peg suits. None of the crowd who were there that day thought about *why* they were there. They had come to the Fewtrells' call, from some of the poorest parts of the city, all of them willing and happy to sustain the injuries and possibly even death at the hands of the Cockney Firm. They had turned up through some sense of loyalty to Birmingham and to each other. None of them took on board that in reality they were there to protect the fortunes of the Fewtrell family and helping them to increase their growing strangle hold over the city.

He told the group of men what they wanted to hear, rousing words of loyalty and reward. Cheers rang out and in Don's rhetoric a time and date was given to them for the battle. A loose arrangement spread throughout the crowd about meeting at the Cedar Club for drinks before and after the scrap. There was no doubt in their minds about the outcome. Unprofessional and untested they may have been, but Birmingham has always created an optimist. There's something to be said of grime and poverty's ability to make a man look for something more than he's born with. Maybe it was just as well they didn't know what was coming along the train tracks, else the optimism would have been drawn out of them like so much hot air.

Drugs-V-Alcohol

Chapter 22

Dixie and Eddie hadn't talked for the past two weeks, but through intermediates Eddie had gotten word to him about the date of the fight and Dixie had arranged with his bosses, to have Snow Hill Railway station shut down on Sunday 14th of October. The whole area was to be cordoned off as a security exercise for a perceived terrorist threat coming from the growing IRA presence in the city. Of course this was all a smoke screen to give the Fewtrells the space needed to send the Krays back to London without any civilian casualties or media interference.

The police were to hold back and not interfere until the fight was over. Dixie's superiors had given him orders to swoop in and nick everyone and anyone involved, including Eddie and his brothers. They saw this as an opportunity to clear the city of these lower class entrepreneurs once and for all and to bring back a bit of decency to the city. All ex army officers, not one of them had a clue how the underworld had changed since the war. Dixie on the other hand was still undecided what he and his serious crime squad were supposed to do, he knew if he nicked everyone his name would be shit on the streets and the leads he'd been fed over the past year or so would soon dry up. Even if he did lose touch with the street he could still follow his orders and climb the career ladder but something in the back of his head kept telling him to stand by the friend he had in Eddie. As the days rolled on Dixie was having difficulties in choosing between the two.

Victoria station hadn't seen such a group on it's platforms since the troops were shipped off to France during the war. Even then the boys of the British expeditionary force were nothing in comparison to the violent characters about to board the North bound train to Birmingham. Neither did they have such an array of weapons at their disposal, all hidden in canvas hold-alls or under camel or leather Crombies, rain coats and jackets. The twins had insisted the men came in small groups and collect on the platform, so as not to draw any more negative attention from the Old Bill and the media.

The atmosphere as the men boarded the train was that of a party as if this were some trip to the seaside instead of the violent battle that lay ahead. Bottles of beer passed from hand to hand along the train and five pint tin barrels were opened with pen knives, the warm beer poured into the little paper cups stolen from the cafes at the station. The Krays and Lambrianous travelled in first class along with their closest associates, drinking the chilled Champagne brought along by Ronnie for the journey. Reggie on the other hand enjoyed making several trips back to the second class carriages to join in the numerous cockney sing-a longs that had begun sporadically along the train. As the beer sank in so the songs and tall stories grew louder and rowdier drowning out the clinking rolling empties that littered the carriage floor. The beer, whisky and gin kept flowing and it seemed like everyone was carrying bottles and by the time they were halfway to Birmingham most were on the wrong side of pissed.

The secrecy they had been so concerned about had all but vanished. Guns were pulled from their hiding places as Flash Harrys stomped up and down the train brandishing whatever weapon they had brought with them. There were even a few pot shots taken at rail signs en route as the party rolled on.

Around four hundred had shown up for the fight. No one seemed to worry about numbers as they all knew the character of the men that were travelling alongside them and counted themselves fortunate just to be included in that number. Spies had been sent to Birmingham but the town had gone quiet. Not a peep had been heard from the Fewtrells since the telephone conversation with Don. So for most of the Londoners travelling north that morning, Birmingham was just a black spot on the map, of no significance or expectation. If things didn't go to plan, not one of them would ever forget the place or indeed set foot there again.

The Cedar club was full to the brim. Maybe six or seven hundred people in there on the Saturday night before the fight. Anyone that wasn't involved in the arrangements for the next day's fun would've noticed that something was in the air. The atmosphere was electric helped along by bags of French blues or yellow Dexondrine which were being handed out willy nilly to anyone that wanted them. Never one for drugs of any sort, Eddie wasn't too happy about them being on the premises but what could he do? These men were here to fight for him, the least he could do was give them a free bar to wash the pills down with. At 2am the regular punters were all kicked out and the scrappers that remained got stuck into the alcohol, not that it made any dent into the speed flowing through their veins. Big Pat was there along with many of the other semi professional boxers and wrestlers from the fighting stables around the city. His huge frame standing a head higher than any other man in the club brought other smaller men gravitating around him, as if his great size would give them some protection in the fight to come.

The Brummies unlike their Cockney counterparts, were taking the whole affair a lot more seriously, partly it must be said due the french blues capacity to sharpen minds. Eddie had organised the scrappers, as he called the non professional villains, into small groups led by the hardest and most trusted of the Whizz Mob. That way anyone who was having second thoughts about fighting and was considering legging it could be given a firm hand and forced to stand their ground.

Eddie also knew Snow Hill station and had chosen his ground well.

He knew they were going to be coming from London with guns amongst other things and he thought he'd found a way to limit their use by using some of the narrow tunnels that separated the different platforms. Only time would tell, and that time was drawing near. Although he felt confident with the turn out, on the negative side the Birmingham IRA hadn't shown up as promised and even though the brothers reassured him that everything would be ok, Eddie spent what was left of the night cursing the Irish for their lack of backbone.

It was with a feeling of dread hanging over him that he saw the first glimmers of the dawn twilight, as they crept through the cracks in the windows to the club and the realisation that the day of the Battle for Birmingham had finally arrived sank in.

Battle Station

Chapter 23

The mood on the train had changed as it pulled into the station. The Krays had to choose two men to go forward into the driver's compartment to make sure the train was ready to leave the station at a moment's notice just in case things went pear shaped. Both Kray brothers cast their eyes over the waiting men, but secretly their decision had already been made. Chris and Anthony Lambrianous were to be left on the train to cover their backs should things go wrong. The Lambrianous brothers protested but the Krays had made up their mind. Their decision wasn't lost on the other members of the Firm, it was a non-violent way to shame the Lambrianous for messing up the hit in the first place. Chris Lambrianous had lost his bottle since the beating in Birmingham so he'd be of no use today anyway.

The few passengers and staff that had had the misfortune to have been traveling on the train that day, had caught on to the fact they were sharing their journey with a bunch of murderous lunatics and were to be found cowering in the forward and rearmost carriages. The train stopped with the deafening creak and squeal of steel against steel making the silence that followed seem all the more oppressive. For a whole minute nothing happened. Eddie and his brothers watched from their secret lookout spot on one of the small steel bridges that crossed the rail tracks. A door sprang open at the front followed shortly by another at the rear of the train. A middle aged woman stepped from the first class carriages and grabbing her son by the hand, hurriedly rushed down the platform as fast a she could, away from the train. Others followed in various states of panic. What must they have thought as they came across the hundreds of men hidden along the train station can only be guessed at. The civilians had all disembarked the train now and still nothing moved on the platform. Eddie was hoping it would stay that way. Maybe the Cockneys hadn't turned up after all. Maybe this was the end of it?

On the train and still out of sight of the waiting Whizz Mob, the Londoners waited for the word to be passed down from the Krays. Most of them were worse for wear from the booze they had consumed and now the first symptoms of hangovers were kicking in. In contrast to the Brummies who were at the peak of their Amphetamine-induced high and to a man were sharp as a pin.

The Fewtrells watched silently, Eddie could hear the rest of the city going about it's business in the distance, totally unaware of the carnage about to take place in the victorian station and he couldn't help thinking about Hazel as his mind wandered back to normal life, beyond the red brick walls and cast iron of the Brunel style station. Suddenly, every door along the train opened simultaneously, then again nothing. Eddie's heart sank. The platform was still. Then as one, the Londoners stepped from the train, filling the platform weapons in hand, and forming themselves into lines of six or seven they waited. Eddie could see from his vantage point that the Londoners were outnumbered but tooled up to a far higher degree than his crew.

Eddie gave the word to Chrissy who in turn legged it along the rail bridge and as arranged the first group of Brummies, numbering between two and three hundred came from underneath the platform, up the stairs leading from the long narrow underpass beneath the railway lines. This group was made up of Birmingham's hardest. It *had* to be. They were going to get the full brunt of the Cockney assault. Big Pat led the way, pick axe handle in hand

and although he was big in comparison to the Brummies, Eddie could see there were men as big if not bigger on the Kray's side.

In a normal fight there's usually words spoken beforehand, insults or barbed comments intended to either give an excuse or soften up their opponent but the Railway platform was silent as the two crews approached each other. The Brummies marched along the concourse until they were only twenty feet from the Londoners. Then the cat calls started.

"Wankers!"

The Cockney accents seemed strange and aggressive to the Birmingham lads.

"Northern facking mankeys, you're gonna get some today, you facking Cants!"

The men at the front of the Cockney line were pointing at individuals in the Brummie group. Big Pat was getting plenty of it.

"Oooowww he's a big lad ain't he?" came a mocking voice. "He ain't gonna be so big when he gets this across his fackin head!" came the reply from down the line. Pat stepped forward.

"Come on then you cockney Bastards!" He shouted in his Birmingham brogue.

"What the fuck did he say?" came another London voice.

"I don't fackin know, I don't speak faking mankey!"

Their mocking laughter finally drove Big Pat over the edge and without any warning he charged at the front line of the London crew. It took them by surprise and the men in the middle of the front line didn't have a chance and were too tightly packed to protect themselves. Big Pat's cherrywood pick axe handle came down square in the middle of the head of the man standing in the centre of the cockney group. The men either side of him were splattered in his blood as he fell to the ground. He lay at his friend's feet, his body shivering, his skull shattered. Their shock didn't last long though and before the opposing Brummies could muster behind big Pat and cross the small space between the gangs, the Londoners were on big Pat en masse. Clubs and knuckle duster punches were raining down on Pat's head and face but still he didn't go down. This encouraged the Brummies and they sprinted screaming at the

London gang. Seeing this the men from London exploded into a whirlwind of weapons and violence. They were real fighters. Their brutal blows brought the young Birmingham men to their senses creating tiny moments of hesitation in the Birmingham ranks, which the Londoners exploited in the most vicious way.

The platform was suddenly turned into a packed blood bath. Anyone that fell didn't get up and it was the Brummies who were falling faster. Some of the men sought space to fight properly by dragging their opponents down off the platform and onto the railway lines, where they could swing their weapons with power.

Eddie, Chrissy and the other Fewtrell brothers watched on from the steel rail bridge as their best were pounded and beaten by London's hardest. He could see the Krays further along the track surrounded by members of the Firm pointing at the individual fights that had started to separate from the main group. Further up the platform at the rear of the gang he saw Ronnie smile and pat his twin on the back as the fight started to flow in the direction of the London mobsters.

All along the platform the Brummies were being pushed back by the onslaught. Big Pat was gone, lost in the melee, unconscious and trodden under foot. Eddie's scrappers began to fall back. The terrible damage from the barbed wire billy clubs and hatchets the cockneys had brought down the line was plain to see. Men flayed and scarred for life, lost ears, eyes, noses and fingers to the lethal weapons. Eddie gave Don the signal for a retreat. Don stood up on the small bridge and gave a blow on the police whistle. The men that weren't involved and trapped in the fight turned and ran back the way they'd came and down the stairs and into the underpass. The unfortunate ones engaged in the fight were left to fend for themselves. The Krays saw this and both Ronnie and Reg began screaming at the gang to give chase.

Ronnie began jumping up and down with excitement. Much to the amazement of the watching Fewtrells Ron drew a long gleaming sword from beneath his long rain coat and began waving it around his head like some modern day cavalry officer. The Birmingham ranks broke completely. Panic ripped through them and they began to leg it as fast as they could, the Cockneys closed in on the poor men left behind, before giving chase.

Scampering down the concrete stairway the mass of Brummies swung right into the underpass that ran beneath the railway line. The further they ran down the tunnel the less panic gripped them, for waiting at the other end of the underpass were 200 hundred or so fresh men that had been stood in silence in reserve since the beginning of the fight. As the men arrived they received pats on the back and smiles. The waiting men could see the look of shock and blood on the faces of their fellow Brummies as they arrived, the sight sending shock waves through the reserve. Some of the younger ones began to talk in low voices amongst themselves about backing out, legging it, but this was cut short by a few cuffs around the ears and strong words by Frankie and Chrissy Fewtrell and the other members of the Whizz Mob.

Eddie knew that the tunnel would take away any advantage the Londoners had over the Brummies by packing them into the underpass. The billy clubs and hatchets that had done so much damage on the platform would be of no use in such a confined space. The Cockneys having finished off the fifty or so men left on the platform began to muster at the top of the stairs. Ron and Reg began making their way to the front of their crew, both of them smelling victory. Reg gave the order.

"Come on then, let's facking finish em off!"

The Firm ran before him descending the stairs as one, screaming bloody murderous obscenities and waving their barbed wired, billy clubs swords and axes above their heads as they gathered speed at the bottom of the stairs. They swung into the tunnel at a full run. The men at the front of the charge could see the Birmingham gang at the other end of the tunnel waiting for them. Still they ran full pelt thinking this was the same lot they had just beaten on the platform above and it wasn't until they were twenty yards or so away from the Brummies that they realised that far from being the defeated men from earlier, this was a new group; fresh eager to fight and all armed with long bladed knives and machetes.

The Londoners at the front of the charge stopped in their tracks, none of them wanting to be the first to be pin cushioned on the long blades of the Brummie's waiting for them. The Cockneys that came behind couldn't see what was waiting at the other end of the tunnel and charged on regardless.The ever growing mass of men pushed forward, much to the protest of the stationary men at the front, their panicked screams drowned out by the Cockney battle cry.

The men at the front went down as the flood of humans pushed forward. The men directly behind them fell on top of their fallen colleagues, and so it went on until the front line of the London crew was just a massive, head high pile of screaming, cursing men trying to extradite themselves from the chaos. The men in the front line were being crushed under the weight of the men on top of them and they in turn were being crushed by the immense pressure still building in the tunnel by the Londoners at the rear, still trying to get into the underpass to the fight. The fortunate ones at the back couldn't see what was happening further down the line and began pushing as hard as they could, thinking that the Birmingham mob were putting up a last ditched effort at the other end of the tunnel and in some way thought that by *pushing* they were helping their fellow gang members defeat their enemy. Far from helping they were contributing to the crush. The mass of men became so tightly packed that the Brummies didn't need to do anything. They just watched, enthralled by the weird horror show that played out before them. Without prompt, one of the Whizz Mob stepped forward, knife in hand. He turned to Chrissy and Frankie Fewtrell.

"Well what are we waiting for? We ain't got all dressed up for nothing, get stuck in lads!"

The man spoke in a matter of fact manner, no emotion in his voice, as if he were about to kill a bag of rats; an unpleasant but necessary job. He turned back to the melee and ran at the mass and began stabbing mercilessly into anything and everything. The men behind him ran forward and followed his example. The sight was horrific. Arms thrust up and down stabbing and slashing into human faces, shoulders, hands, or whatever the crushed men tried to protect themselves with. Agonising, blood-curdling screams and squeals of terribly injured men rang out through the tunnel and still the push from the Cockney end continued. Stab! Stab! Stab! The Brummie knives searched for new victims. The Whizz Mob men stood on the fallen Londoners agonised and trapped bodies in order to reach further into the mass of men trapped deep in the crush.

From his vantage point Eddie could see the Cockney crew waiting to get into the tunnel. Don appeared and told him what the situation was in the underpass. This was his chance to outflank the Londoners! He could see Ron and Reg standing at the bottom of the stairs yelling at the Firm members to push harder. Eddie had to grab this opportunity now, before the Krays realised what was happening in the tunnel. He ran down to the Brummie end of the tunnel. He could see his crew waiting to get into the fight, groups of them peering over each other's shoulders trying to see what was happening in the tunnel. Eddie grabbed at the men pulling them away from the crowd, his other brothers helping him.

"Come on, we'll go up onto this platform, cross the railway line and trap them at the bottom of the stairs in the tunnel!" Word passed along to the members of the Whizz mob that couldn't fit into the tunnel to follow Eddie. The group followed him up the stairs and onto the platform running parallel to the one the Cockneys occupied. They jumped down into the pit containing the railway tracks, and some of their unconscious fellow scrappers, left there earlier by the London gang.

Eddie, Don, the other brothers and about one hundred of the Whizz Mob raced across the space separating the platforms. As Eddie and his brothers reached the other side many of the Brummies were still climbing down from the platform onto the tracks. Just as Eddie began to climb onto the platform controlled by the Krays, a Cockney voice rang out a warning. The voice belonged Anthony Lambrianous who could see the Brummies from his vantage point in the driver's compartment on the train. He was shouting to Reg who was standing at the top of the staircase above the chaos below. Reg turned to the see where the voice was coming from. Instantly he saw the flood of Brummies crossing the line.

"Ronnie get the fuck up here now!"

Ronnie appeared at the top of the stairs with a large green canvas bag in hand. He summed up the situation in the blink of an eye and dropping the bag he and Reg both dug into the holdall and pulled out two small black Sten machine guns. Eddie watched helpless and in horror as the twins loaded the long black magazines into the side of the weapons almost simultaneously and stepped towards the rail pit. The Whizz Mob crossing the rails were caught in the open only Eddie and his brothers had made it to the other side. Eddie stood there frozen as the Kray twins brought the barrels of the small black machine guns to point directly at him. Recognition suddenly lit up Ron's face as he stared at Eddie, his eyes grew wide as he placed Eddie's face to the meeting at the Bermuda club all those many months before, the moment this whole affair had started. To his left Reggie opened fire on the men in the pit. Firing over Eddie and his brothers heads the little bullets ripped into the hard standing on the pit floor sending stone chipping's and shrapnel into the men's legs and feet. Luckily for the Brummies caught in the open, the Sten machine gun was notoriously inaccurate. The little gun sprayed its bullets in just over two seconds until it's magazine was empty leaving ten or so men clutching their bleeding lower legs. The burst of gun ire was short yet brutal and it had stopped the flood of men across the rail pit. Reggie dropped to his knees and searched the bag for another mag of bullets. Ronnie still hadn't fired. He was caught in a moment with Eddie.

For the two men, time froze. The nano seconds it took for Ronnie to recognise Eddie seemed to slow down with each heart beat, bringing time to a halt. Eddie saw Ronnie's face turn from anger to rage, his hand slowly pulling back the cocking bar on the black Sten gun. Eddie was caught in the sights and there was nothing to be done. He'd given it his best shot but the Krays had him now and in those few tiny moments he accepted his death at the hands of Ronnie Kray. Eddie braced himself for the bullets to strike him down, grimmacing, he closed his eyes and waited for death. They say that life passes before you in the moments before meeting your maker and for Eddie this was certainly true. His mind ran over the first meeting with the Krays, the shooting of the bear, Jack and the Lambrianous and Hazel's face. All these images from the past months ran through his mind in a blur of different emotions. He offered himself to the gun shots about to kill him, but nothing came. He came back to his senses when he heard the crack as a bullet whizzed passed his ear. He opened his eyes and the sight before him added to his confusion, instead of the Krays aiming their machine guns at point blank range, he saw the grey platform around Ron and Reg suddenly explode into a shower of concrete chippings as bullets sprayed around them. The twins were caught for a split second in a bizarre dance of death as the bullets peppered the platform and wooden benches behind them. The two men were caught completely by surprise by the hail. The back of Ron's long beige rain coat was now full of little holes but miraculously neither him nor his twin were hit. Eddie stood there stupidly trying to work out what the hell was happening when Don grabbed his arm and pulled him to down onto the hard standing.

"Get down ya silly bastard the IRA are here!" Eddie looked around him. Chrissy and Don were sheltering next to the rails beneath the platform's over hang. On the other platform a group of five men stood in line. All of them had flat caps and black scarves around their faces making them appear like something from an old western movie with only their eyes showing, completely disguising them. In their hands were what looked like brand new Thompson sub-machine guns. Only two of them were firing, two others stood and aimed but held their fire and the fifth covered the rest of the station. They had an air of professionalism about them, obviously disciplined and trained to cover each other, these five IRA men now controlled the fight completely. A cheer came up from the other Brummie men caught in the rail pit as they made their escape under cover of the Irish. Eddie slapped his brothers arms and laughed.

"The fucking Irish have turned up!" Laughing with relief

"Go on you Irish bastards give em some shit." Don joined in laughing hysterically. Chrissy looked horrified.

"Shut up you silly cunt or they'll start shooting us as well!"

The Krays didn't know what hit them. Ron and Reg raced back to the train for cover from the bullets. They hadn't planned on the IRA being involved, although it must be said at this stage they didn't know who these men were. All they knew was that they were out gunned and this was the end of the fight. The only thing that mattered now was to get out alive and with as many of the Firm as they could muster. Reg gave the order to the Lambrianous in the driver's compartment to sound the train horn. Suddenly a deafening siren filled the station, drowning out the machine guns and shouting from the tunnel. The Cockneys still pushing and fighting in the underpass heard the siren. They all knew the pre-arranged signal and when the horn blew they had only a minute or so before the train would pull out. If they weren't on it they'd be on their own and the thought of being left in Birmingham with these savages wasn't one the Londoners relished. As the men at the rear of the crush retreated up the stairs towards the train so the men further in the tunnel began to have some space and the extradite themselves from the chaos. Some of the older Cockneys pulled their friends and in some cases family from the pile of squashed humans still trapped in the centre of the underpass and slowly the crush abated. Frankie Fewtrell guessed what was happening and shouted at the Brummies to let the Londoners free themselves.

The Whizz Mob members stood back and waited to see what would happen, but it was plain that the cockneys had had enough. Many of the men who seconds before had been caught in the crush were now free and a general panic set in amongst the Londoners. Men with awful knife wounds to their necks, heads, hands and arms suddenly full of life as adrenaline gave them the energy for self preservation, driving them back up the stairs and to the safety aboard the train. Men were still running along the platform as the great metal wheels of the locomotive made a huge cracking sound as the train slowly came to life. Carriage doors swung open as the men inside tried to help their fellow wounded aboard where they collapsed exhausted and in shock. The Kray brothers walked the carriages taking in the carnage around them as the train moved backwards out of Snow Hill station. They stepped over the men that only an hour before had been drunkenly singing and boasting about their prowess in the fighting world, were now mostly torn suits and blood. The brothers talked in soft tones to each other, pushing down the defeat, they went over what this would mean if the story got out around the other gangs of the East End. Little did they know at the time that this was to be the first of many such battles that would be fought and eventually lost by the new princes of London. They didn't know it but the writing was on the wall for the twins and their eventual and infamous down fall was only a few years away.

The Brummies had emerged from the tunnel and were now stood on the other platform. Just as many of them had been injured, some simply sat in groups on the cold concrete like school kids and watched as the train pulled away. Eddie and his brothers joined the main group as the train now gathering speed reversed out of the station. Eddie searched the crowd but couldn't see the IRA. He pushed his way through the crowd and just caught sight of the five men disappearing down some stairs at the other end of the platform. One of them stopped and took off his flat cap. A shock of blonde hair was all Eddie could see, the black scarf covering the rest of his face. The two men stared at each other for a few seconds then the IRA man gave a small salute and was gone.

A screeching sound brought Eddie back to the moment and he turned to see the London train depart. One or two arms coming out of the train windows from the Londoners who still had fight in them giving wanker signs as the train left but these were answered with loud cheers from the Whizz Mob and just like that, the battle for Birmingham was over.

All in all it had been a close call with five men dead, two Londoners and three Whizz mob members two more would later die from their injures and about one hundred badly wounded but who would live. There was still some Cockneys in the tunnel, many of whom were unconscious, but the fight was over now and they were helped, without prejudice, back to their feet or dragged along the concourse to where they could get some medical attention from the police who had now started to show up en masse. Big Pat was being attended to by his friends. The gargantuan of a man had a huge gash across his forehead, but apart from that, he was fine. Eddie caught his eye and the two men nodded in approval to each other. Dixie walked across the platform, a big grin on his face and hugged Eddie.

"You fucking did it our kid you beat em ha hay." He slapped the tops of Eddie's arms excitedly like a child but instead of smiling back Eddie gave Dixie a look of concern.

"They nearly had us Dixie. No doubt about it, them Cockney boys are hard bastards. Got to give em the respect they deserve. The Krays had me in their sights point blank. They would've beat us if it weren't for the IRA jumping in." Dixie's smile dropped.

"The IRA were here? Well where are they now? Those Irish fuckers need to be brought in Ed."

Eddie looked at Dixie straight in the eye.

"Look all I know is we asked the Irish to help keep the Krays out of Brum and true to their word they stepped in when it looked like it was going tits up. If you want to nick em then you carry on, but let me tell you this. If it weren't for the IRA we wouldn't be having this conversation now, I'd be dead and you'd have to deal with Ronnie or Reg Kray, your magical rise to the top of the police force would be over pal."

Dixie nodded, he turned and scanned the station for any sign of the IRA men but they were long gone. He knew they would just sink back into the Irish quarter in Digbeth never to be seen again. The machine guns would be cleaned and stored in cellars or lofts until they were needed again for the Irish uprising the top brass had been warning about for years.

Dixie became serious.

"You and your lads had best fuck off sharpish!" He said matter of factually,

"The top brass are on their way down here now and want plenty of arrests. Anyone that still here in five minutes will be nicked!" Eddie turned to Chrissy.

"Pass the word along we gotta move out of here now! No fucking around, tell em all we'll meet at the Cedar club. Anyone too hurt can get a taxi to the hospital on me." Dixie butted in.

"Tell anyone from the Whizz Mob to go to Selly Oak hospital. *Don't* use the QE that's where we are gonna take anyone we nick. If any of your lot show up there they'll get nicked Ed, it'll be out of my hands at that point. "

Eddie pointed at the dead men. Their bodies had been laid out on the platform in a line, faces covered with jackets.

"What about them?" Dixie gave Eddie a smile.

"I've already thought of that, they are gonna be taken to the Q.E too. This lot are gonna help science." Eddie looked confused. Dixie continued.

"These young men have heroically donated their bodies to the future of man kind." Still non plussed, Eddie waited for a better explanation.

"Dissected you thick cunt. They're gonna be chopped up . . . legally . . . by doctors, it's the best way of getting rid of them without too many questions."

Even as they spoke the policemen under Dixie's command were moving the bodies into black rubber body bags and carrying them into the waiting black mariah.

Eddie wasn't happy about it but nodded, he patted Dixie's arm and walked away without another word. Dixie was happy they were talking again. He was going to ignore his bosses on the force. Yes he would make arrests but they would be arrests with London accents. He wouldn't nick a Brummie, he couldn't, this was his city now and he had to make a name for himself in it. He was in with a man that was going somewhere and he wanted it to stay that way. The Birmingham underworld was about to explode and Dixie had got himself right at the epicentre

Eddie and the rest of the Fewtrell brothers made their way back to the Cedar Club with anyone still able to walk. He felt a weight lifted from his shoulders, and for the thirty minutes it took to walk back to the club, his paranoia had left him completely. He was the boss now. No one was above him. No more dogs nipping his heels, he was top dog in the city and he was going to hold on to that as long as he possibly could, whatever it took.

Hazel, George and were waiting for Eddie and his brothers at the Cedar club. All were relieved at the outcome of the battle. Eddie grabbed Hazel and pulled her into him and held her, the memory of the gun barrel pointing at him point blank, still fresh in his mind. He didn't think he would ever see her again.

As the Whizz Mob members began to arrive in small groups, a spontaneous celebration began and the beginnings of a brotherhood had begun. Drinks were poured and the party started to take on a life of its own. Jackie Diamond had resurfaced along with his French accent, taking great pride in showing anyone who was interested the long scar across his throat, left there by the Lambrianou brothers. His survival had made him even more flamboyant than he was before the attack, but any ideas he had of running a night club were long forgotten.As more and more men turned up at the club Eddie whispered to Hazel to start charging for the drinks. Hazel couldn't believe he was going to charge these fighters for drinks after what they had done for him, but she kept her feelings to herself.

The drinking went on well into Monday morning with the men recounting their brave deeds performed that day in battle, mostly just boasting, bluff and banter but although it was never said openly, everyone there acknowledged Eddie Fewtrell as the new King of Birmingham.

Eddie drank with the men, wandering from group to group listening and boasting, patting backs. Even though he was surrounded by people laughing and drinking he felt something new, a fearful hollow feeling that seemed to grow stronger by the hour, a feeling that *all* Kings throughout history have experienced. For the first time in his life he felt truly alone. He had climbed to the top of the mountain, only to find out there was only room for one at the top, and in that moment he knew that like the Kings of old, he would spend the rest of his days searching in the shadows of his kingdom for betrayal and treason amongst his enemies, friends and family.

Epilogue

The phone gave a trill that rang throughout the great entrance hall, the sound bouncing off the cold marble tiles that lined the floor to the Mayfair mansion. The butler crossed the room, back straight and expressionless, picking the phone up in almost military precision. "Hello, Lord Boothby's residence. Who may I say is calling?"

"Tell him it's Ronnie," came the Cockney voice on the other end of the line. The butler left the phone and went to fetch his master. After a short while Lord Boothby picked up the receiver.

"Ronnie my dear boy, how can I help you this evening?"

There was a short silence then . . . "I need to come over . . . I've had a really bad week." The man's voice sounded drawn and heavy on the line. Boothby could hear a labour to Ronnie's breathing. "I need to let off a bit of steam, maybe play with one of your puppies?" "I thought we had agreed that you stay away Ronnie old chap." Boothby let the words hang and waited for Ronnie's reply for a second, but nothing came, instead he thought he heard sobbing from the gangster. Finally Ronnie spoke.

"Nah I'm not finished with you yet, I gotta see you." Boothby took control.

"Ronnie dear boy, you know I'm fond of you but . . . things have changed. You need to understand that I am Lord Boothby and I am the one that says when things are finished, not you." Boothby looked for words. "Let me explain in a way you'll understand. You see Ronnie, when a bow is drawn and let's the arrow fly, the arrow has all the promise of hitting its target, but, if the arrow misses its target, . . . well then one loses all interest in that arrow and one invariably moves onto the next dart." He let Ronnie have a few seconds to work out the analogy before continuing. "You were very entertaining for a while Ronnie, but the Westminster jungle drums are banging their rhythms loud and clear my dear boy, storm clouds are gathering for you and Reginald and people like myself cant afford to be caught out in the rain with people like you." At that moment he was joined by middle aged, plump, grey haired man, who crossed the room and held his hand. "I'm going to go now Ronnie," . . . more sobbing on the line, Boothby continued. "Act like a gentleman and *don't* call again!" He placed the receiver down and turned to the man next to him. "Those two Kray boys are getting a little too big for their boots, be a darling and sort it out would you. Get some of your people from special branch to get this problem behind bars, once and for all." He stroked the man's cheek. "After all you're probably going to become the next leader of the Tory party, and what's the point in that if you cant pull a few strings."

The two men returned to the party hand in hand.

The man from the East

On the 21st of May 1967, a young family arrived from Pakistan at the newly fitted out airport on the Coventry Road Birmingham. The father carried his young son on his shoulder down the steps from the plane and across the tarmac where he was met by his brother, cousins and other family and friends all welcoming him to his new life in Birmingham.

His name was Zaffa Iqbal. The youngest member of the Iqbal family who belong to the lower cast group from Peshawar region. Penniless but proud, he had worked as a private driver for his rich benefactor until Zaffa, having taken enough of his bosses insults decided to smash the arrogant bastards head in with a tire iron. Taking his money and selling the car he left Pakistan as fast as he could, with no morals to trouble his mind he had money and a plan.

He had seen his boss selling the pretty prostitutes high on Afghanistan heroin on the streets and now he would do the same in England. Rich fat white people would pay to fuck *his* girls in *his* brothels and take the drugs procured and smuggled into Birmingham by his contacts in Afghanistan and Birmingham airport. He was here to make his mark on the world. His hand would deal out the payback that Britain had brought upon his country. He would use the same things the British had employed on his people.

Blackmail, torture and murder, all just tools given him by Allah to destroy anyone that stood in his way. He was going to shake up this city by bringing the will of Allah down on the heads of the infidels and give it something it had never had before.

A Pakistani King.

www.accidentalgangster.com

Printed in Great Britain
by Amazon